"I'll make you admit that you love me, Melly."

Trent's arrogance fired Melly's anger. "If I lose my head over you again, what happens then?"

He turned his head so that his lips touched her hair. "Oh, Melly. How can I tell you you're all I ever wanted?"

The ragged note in his voice caught at her heart. But only for a moment. "Remember, you told me that three years ago. A month later I was reading a letter from you, which said you hoped I hadn't read too much into a declaration made in the heat of the moment."

Melly thought her anger hid the desolation she'd felt, but he groaned, "Hell, did you really think I'd forgotten? I wrote exactly the sort of letter I thought would make you hate me."

Why? her mind screamed.

ROBYN DONALD, her husband and their two children make their home in the far north of New Zealand where they indulge their love for outdoor life in general and sailing in particular. She keeps a file of clippings, photographs and a diary that, she confides, "is useful in my work as well as for settling family arguments!"

Books by Robyn Donald

These books may be available at your local bookseller.

Don't miss any of our special offers. Write to us at the following address for information on our newest releases.

Harlequin Reader Service
901 Fuhrmann Blvd., P.O. Box 1397, Buffalo, NY 14240
Canadian address: P.O. Box 603,
Fort Erie, Ont. L2A 9Z9

ROBYN DONALD

long journey back

Harlequin Books

TORONTO • NEW YORK • LONDON
AMSTERDAM • PARIS • SYDNEY • HAMBURG
STOCKHOLM • ATHENS • TOKYO • MILAN

For Des, who found Brian,
And for Brian, who knows all about perfidy
in the electronics industry,

Many thanks.

Harlequin Presents first edition December 1986
ISBN 0-373-10936-9

Original hardcover edition published in 1986
by Mills & Boon Limited

CHAPTER ONE

THE TOWERS, a large, extremely luxurious apartment block which housed the Hollingworth family when they came to Auckland, was built on a lower slope of one of the small volcanoes which are such a feature of the isthmus.

They looked, Melly Hollingworth decided as she stood at the window overlooking it, as though some giant toddler has gone mad with a bucket and spade.

Certainly the one she was admiring was shaped exactly like a sandcastle. Green and steep and sharp, the grassy slopes lifted up towards a sky shaded with the purple of fast-approaching twilight. For a landscape which had had a violent and fiery genesis it breathed calm and serenity, helped by the sheep that meandered silently across its slopes and the frill of large old trees at its base.

Melly sighed, but terminated the sigh with guilty determination. She was *happy*! Only two minutes ago over the telephone she had assured her half-sister most fervently that she was happy, even elated. Why should she not be? Yesterday she had learned that her application for what looked to be a stimulating and fascinating new job had been accepted. When she had returned to New Zealand she had not expected to be able to make use of her experience of the previous two years which she had spent working for a big firm in London as their librarian. It had to be good fortune of the highest order which had led to an opening so like her previous position just when she was ready to start looking for a job.

So, her professional life was set fair. She was happy

to be back home after almost three years in exile, she
was free and twenty-four and the trust fund her father
Dougal Hollingworth had set up for her provided an
income higher than she would ever need. She had a
loving half-brother, the only son of her father, and a
loving half-sister, the only daughter of her mother's first
marriage before she had met and fallen in love with
Dougal. After years spent apart, Rafe and Jennet had
met, fallen in love, married and produced a gorgeous
nephew also called Dougal for Melly to adore.

She smiled, thinking of his cheerful babble on the
telephone a few minutes before. Already she missed his
sticky kisses and enchanting mischief. Still, she
reminded herself firmly, she would be seeing him again
at Christmas, only a month away. And that was
another blessing to count. It was early summer, and
outside The Towers the air was fresh and warm with a
hint of the drowsiness of high summer.

Definitely she was happy. Already her network of
friends was enmeshing her into the round of pre-
Christmas festivities. She need never be lonely. There
was no place for self-pity in her life.

So she walked into her bedroom, to pull on a pair of
shorts over legs whose tan originated from the
exceptionally good summer experienced in the northern
hemisphere, enhanced by long afternoons spent by the
pool at Te Puriri, Rafe's station in the north. A T-shirt
fitted closely over breasts slightly too ample to be stylish.

'Thank heavens I'm tall,' she told her reflection,
yanking the shirt past her unfashionably narrow waist.

Once Rafe had told her that she had an Edwardian
body without the S-bend! Hours of eyeing her reflection
when in the turmoil of adolescence had forced her to
accept his judgment, but she was still not entirely
resigned to it.

'Oh well,' she said aloud now, 'at least I've got long
legs. And a flat backside.'

Which, in part, made up for those curving hips.

The grounds were cared for by an inspired and devoted gardener who manicured lawns and was lovingly ruthless in his attendance on flower borders and the shrubbery. Because of its position the big building had an air of being in the country. As she jogged briskly down the drive Melly took deep breaths of air that was fresh and sweet with the perfume of flowers, the sounds of traffic almost drowned by the rhythmic 'tock' of tennis balls and laughter and splashing from the pool.

Carefully, pacing herself to prevent any over-tiredness, she ran out of the gates with their notice warning of the security patrol and up the road to the little park beneath great silvery olive trees and a few splendid Empress trees with their clusters of blossoms like enormous mauve foxgloves. In the canopy of a huge idesia last year's berries gleamed scarlet-orange among the tender brilliance of the new leaves.

Melly felt an upwelling of delight, of joy in the responses of her strong young body and that exquisite pleasure that comes from arriving home after a long and weary journey. She smiled at other runners, at a couple walking a tiny, alert apricot poodle, at a pair of lovers wandering along hand in hand.

At last, flushed and sweaty, she headed back through the long shadows. As she walked through the main doors she wondered idly if perhaps she might spend the rest of this tender, evocative twilight swimming off the restlessness she should have burned out running.

Like everything else about The Towers, the lobby was luxurious and well organised, but not even the best of architects could prevent a situation when the doors were closing on one lift and the other one was almost at the very top of the building.

It was hopeless, but automatically Melly lengthened her stride, muttering beneath her breath. Normally she would not have cared about waiting, but the flush brought on by her exercise was fading now and the air struck chill against her heated skin. And perhaps that inner restlessness which had her in its grip explained the frown which drew her black brows together.

She had already stopped and turned to the next lift when she heard the sound of the doors behind her re-opening. Whoever was in there must have seen her and was politely stopping for her. Her slow, beautiful smile irradiated her face as she hurried between the doors, conscious of a slight touch of impatience in the tall man who waited, a finger on the control panel.

'Thank you . . .' Her voice jolted, then died away as she turned her head to meet ice-grey eyes, cool and dispassionate, as hard as quartz.

'Hello, Melissa,' Trent Addison said calmly as he pressed the button. 'How long have you been back?'

He knew, she thought, dazed eyes fixed on the panel. He hadn't needed to ask which floor. For a moment she was so stunned that she had to lean back against the wall while the roaring in her head cleared. It was anger which saved her from the humiliation of fainting, anger at the machinations of a Fate which had meddled too often in their affairs and seemed determined to begin all over again.

Swallowing hard to ease her dry mouth and throat, she turned away from his open appraisal and answered woodenly, 'Over a month. Almost six weeks.'

He tilted his head to watch the lighted numbers flashing on and off. A slight smile gave his harsh features a saturnine cast. 'I was up at Te Puriri,' she added, as though it mattered.

He knew that, too, her reply was no surprise to him. The thin mouth curled in a not particularly pleasant smile. 'Staying with your brother and sister.'

'Half-brother and half-sister,' Melly corrected swiftly, then bit her lip. The correction had been automatic, caused by the number of times she had had to explain to the curious that although Rafe was her half-brother and Jennet her half-sister they were not related to each other by blood.

But Trent knew all about the tangled relationships in her family; in a way, he was almost one of them.

He nodded, heavy-lidded eyes narrowed as they roved the dark curls about her face before moving down to capture her eyes.

'In these days of divorce and re-marriage complicated families are almost the norm,' he remarked idly, 'but I must admit it's the first time I've known a stepbrother and sister marrying each other. I believe they have a son.'

Her tense expression softened, warmed, as she thought of her nephew. 'Yes,' she said with immense satisfaction.

The faint 'ting' of the lift bell announcing their arrival brought her back to reality. Her floor, thank God. As the doors whispered open she lied with a quite shattering banality, 'Nice to see you again,' and hurried out without a backward glance, her whole body clenching in pain.

Her running shoes made no sound as she sped across the carpet to her door. Behind her she heard the doors of the lift close and almost sagged with relief, fumbling in her pocket for the key. Her fingers trembled as she inserted it; the faint sound of the mechanism was hidden by another which brought her twisting around, her eyes dilated.

'Calm down,' Trent ordered, that silvery gaze impaling her like a sacrifice against the door.

'Do you live here?' she asked raggedly, then flushed at the inanity of the question. 'I mean—on this floor? Next door?'

'No, on the floor above.' A lean brown hand turned the handle of the door and opened it behind her.

Smiling down into her incredulous face he said blandly, 'I live in the penthouse, Melissa.'

She backed in, her whole attention bent on him as he followed her, and closed the door behind them. 'Then what are you doing? What do you want?'

Trent had thin brows, beautifully shaped; he used them with devastating effect, as now, when the fraction of an upward movement made her feel gauche and stupid.

'We do know each other,' he reminded her with gentle insolence, his mild tone failing entirely to hide the note of sarcasm in his deep, rather gravelly voice. 'Quite well, in fact. At one time, between your engagement to my cousin Derek and your visit overseas, well enough to talk seriously about marriage. Why shouldn't I come in and have a cup of coffee with you, catch up on the past three years?'

'Merely the fact that you married Cathy Durrant instead of me,' she returned, her fragile equilibrium swamped by a black fury that flamed in her eyes, then died away, leaving behind only the ashes of a dead love.

The brilliant clarity of his gaze didn't alter, but the strong bone structure of his face seemed to harden. It was an optical illusion brought about by her pain and disillusion, for within a second it was gone and he gave a lazy, cynical smile.

'Hell hath no fury like a woman scorned,' he said lightly. 'Well, I suppose I deserve it, although I'd hoped that during the last three years you'd have lost that juvenile tendency to see everything in shades of black and white. Did you know that Cathy and I are divorced?'

'Yes.' Her beautifully shaped mouth curled. 'You split up immediately Sir Peter Durrant died, I believe.'

An odd little silence stretched between them, dangerous, shivering with tension.

Trent broke it by saying silkily, 'We made it official a

month later, but yes, Cathy went to stay with Lady Durrant the day after he died. How depressing to find that you have a mind commonplace enough to give credence to that sort of gossip.'

She smiled, a cold, proud little movement of stiff lips. 'I still have this juvenile tendency to believe the evidence of my eyes,' she said, mocking him. 'If that's gossip, then I'm sorry to disappoint you, but yes, I believe it.'

'Yet I'd have thought that your experience with Derek would have persuaded you that the evidence of your eyes need not necessarily be true.'

Melly winced, the colour fleeing her skin so that for a moment she looked sallow. During her engagement to Derek she had been completely unaware of the dark core of violence in him until he had been goaded into losing control and attacking her. Trent had played some part in the goading, for Derek had been his cousin.

Defensively she protested, 'That was—different.'

'Of course,' he said politely, his eyes peculiarly bleak as if he were looking at some intensely painful vision.

Her mouth tightened as her head went up. 'Very well then, tell me,' she invited, not angrily, allowing only irony to be revealed in expression and tone. 'Did you marry Cathy Durrant because you loved her, Trent?'

The heavy lids narrowed his eyes into long streaks of silver, opaque and burnished. 'No,' he said uncompromisingly.

'And do you now control her grandfather's, Sir Peter's, holdings?'

Beside his hard mouth a muscle flicked, then was brought under control. 'Yes.'

'And were you sorry when she went back to live with Lady Durrant after her grandfather died?'

He leaned back against the closed door, arms folded over the broad chest. A pirate's smile just touched his mouth, reckless, ruthless, and that aura of danger crackled about him. Melly felt a sudden surge of adrenalin which helped in her refusal to be intimidated as she held his gaze defiantly with her own.

'No,' he said deliberately. 'I was glad to see her go.'

It hurt. After three years it still hurt to have every obscene rumour confirmed, but time had given her practice in hiding the pain. So she took a deep shuddering breath and fought it down, her shock at this sudden, unwanted reunion fading now.

'Perhaps there was a reason—other than the one that leaps to mind—for your marriage,' she suggested with frigid sarcasm.

Beneath the superbly tailored jacket of his suit his shoulders lifted in the slightest of shrugs. 'Would you believe one?'

'It would have to be good.'

For a moment he seemed to hesitate, that keen buccaneer's face sharpening. His eyes lanced across her scornful expression, probing, dissecting. Then he repeated that tiny shrug and a curtain of impassivity seemed to hide his reactions. Blandly he said, 'Sorry, my sweet one, I'm not into giving excuses, not even if they're true. I have this intuitive suspicion that whatever I told you would be disbelieved.'

Until that moment Melly hadn't realised how intensely she had yearned for him to give her some reason for so cruelly jilting her. The disappointment was intolerable, unbearable; it was all she could do to retain some sort of control so that she did not display her emotions like a side-show for his amusement.

Terrified at the strength of her reaction, she astounded herself by producing a smile. It wasn't up to her usual standard but close enough to fool most people. 'You're probably right. So . . .?'

Trent ignored her gesture towards the door. In the darkness of his face the white slash of his grin was dangerous, almost feral. He looked like a hunter presented at last with prey worthy of him.

'I'd like that cup of coffee.' And as she began to protest he laid a long, imperative finger over her mouth. 'Why not?'

'Because I—we . . .' Her indignant words trailed into silence as she became aware of his glance at her mouth. Immediately she was assailed by sensation; the warmth of his finger against her lips, the sensuous way the nerve-endings in those most sensitive of features responded to the light pressure against them. A slow trickle of heat inched its way up from the centre of her body. She had forgotten, she thought, her mind in confusion. Her eyes clung to his, unable to move even when she recognised the quick blaze of attraction which lit them from behind.

Then he removed his finger, stepping back. Suddenly cold, she bit her lip, hating him for the almost contemptuous ease with which he inflamed her responses. Would it never die, that insidious, frightening flare-up of the senses, all-pervasive and ravishingly seductive?

In a voice that almost trembled she said coldly, 'Please go, Trent. I'm sticky and tired, I want to shower and go to bed.'

'No problem. Show me where the kitchen is and I'll make the coffee.'

'Can't you understand? I don't want to have you here!'

'Tough,' he said, then laughed at the unhidden anger he saw in her expression. 'I love the way your eyes glitter like black diamonds when you're furious. Don't you think you're over-reacting? Are you afraid of me? Or of my effect on you?'

'Don't try to manipulate me!' she gritted.

'Why not? You react so superbly. No, no, don't go all outraged. I won't let you hit me, so don't even try it. Accept the inevitable, Melissa. You're not strong enough to push me out of the door and I promise to go once I've had my coffee. You know, you're making so much fuss a man could be forgiven for thinking that you're still just a tiny bit in love with him.'

To hear it said struck a raw nerve. It wasn't true, she no longer felt anything but contempt for him, but for a second she could have killed him as he stood there smiling down at her.

'I'd have to be a masochist,' she said unevenly. 'I doubt if I ever loved you.'

'No?' Those brows winged upwards, expressing a nice blend of sardonic disbelief and scorn.

'No!'

He laughed again and turned her around with a careless hand on her shoulder. 'Well, perhaps you're right. In that case, I needn't feel any guilt for breaking your heart, need I? Now show me where the kitchen is and I'll put the percolator on.'

One of Melly's assets was the ability to know when she was beaten, and cut her losses accordingly. Clearly, for whatever reason, Trent had no intention of going until he'd had his wretched cup of coffee. So she said crisply, 'Oh, you're impossible!' and led the way into the kitchen.

Once there, it was easier for her to set the percolator going, although Trent was more than capable of managing. She remembered from the past how competent he was, with an affinity for machines. He had, she recalled, been brought up by a mother who was fluttery and inclined to invalidism, which possibly explained his efficiency in the kitchen.

'There,' she said, dragging her mind away from the vision of Trent as a schoolboy, lean and gangling yet with the promise of his present lithe grace implicit. 'That's done. I'll go and change. I won't be long.'

She was away just long enough to shower and wash her hair, towel-drying the thick curls as she fought down the impulse to use the hair-drier. How she looked to Trent Addison didn't worry her. Not a bit, she decided as she pulled on a spare silk dress in her favourite shade of apricot. Nor did she use her perfume, but she did lightly colour her lips with the excuse that people with her golden tan looked sallow without lipstick. It could have even been true; quite often was, but in the mirror her eyes avoided the warm colour which emphasised her high cheekbones and the glitter of gold in the black depths of her eyes.

When she emerged Trent had just poured coffee into mugs and was standing by the sink looking out over the lights of Auckland, the electric light gleaming on the mahogany highlights in his hair. The kitchen was not large but it was not small either, yet he seemed to fill it. He had presence, the kind of instant visual impression which had little to do with physical attributes, nothing to do with rank or wealth. She had seen a small, ugly millionaire with it, and a stooped old man who had never possessed enough money to marry. It was power, she thought confusedly, an inner power that was immediately recognisable on the rare occasions one met it. It caught the eye and tantalised the mind and demanded attention. She should be accustomed to it, for her brother had it, yet her breath hurt in her lungs and she felt an eerie lifting of every hair on her skin as he turned.

'Do you still drown it with milk?' he asked after a long, impassive appraisal.

'Yes. Thank you. Come into the drawing-room, it's more comfortable.' The stilted words filled in the awkward tense silence as she led the way.

'Clever,' he remarked, looking around the room. 'Who designed it? It's too personal to be a decorator.'

'Jennet. She's very artistic, very talented. She pots, too. That's one of her pieces over there.'

He cast a cursory look at the beautiful bowl. Melly saw the admiration and opened her mouth for more babble, but the words died on her tongue as his gaze came back to meet hers. Beneath the heavy, straight lashes his eyes were clear and coldly dispassionate with no emotion but a sardonic amusement in them.

'Tell me what you've been up to since last we met,' he commanded softly.

He had all the effrontery in the world. How could he stand there so brazenly asking her what she had been doing? What did he expect? The truth, that she had been mourning her heart's betrayal, constructing defences high and thick so that she would never again have to cope with that numbing despair? Or what?

'Sit down,' she said, sinking into a chair. As he followed suit she drank some coffee to gain time, watching from beneath her long lashes, comparing her memories with the reality. He looked older, as though the past three years had drained him of some of his youth. He wasn't handsome. He had irregular features, an arrogantly hooked nose, a mouth both wide and thin-lipped, a jaw which even with his head lowered was forceful and thrusting; no, he was far from handsome.

But then he didn't need to be. He had style. And, Melly thought as he leaned back into the armchair, settling his wide shoulders against the pale fabric, a more than usual amount of what Diana, her mother, coyly referred to as sex-appeal, a raw, animal vitality which the dark business suit couldn't diminish. Displaying no bulging muscles, no evident signs of the whipcord strength she knew he possessed, his appearance warned of stamina and power and force.

Power. That word again. So many kinds of power, the power to delight the eye, the power to impress the mind.

Melly had never seen a man more good to look at then her half-brother, yet her appreciation of his severe masculine beauty did not lessen the impact of the man who seemed engrossed in his coffee opposite her. As her gaze roamed covertly over him she realised with a tremor of cold fear that while she no longer loved him, and certainly could never again trust him, she still found him potently attractive.

'Well?' he asked, not troubling to hide his mocking smile as he caught her watching him. 'How did you enjoy wallowing in the fleshpots of the Riviera with the beauteous Diana?'

'I spent most of the time in London,' she snapped back stiffly. He had no right to sneer at her mother.

He knew, of course, he didn't even try to fake interest or surprise. Well, it wouldn't have been all that difficult to keep tabs on her, she wrote to several people in Auckland, at least two of whom moved in the same circles as Trent.

But he prompted blandly, 'Doing what?'

'I worked in the library at Inco.'

'Enjoy it?'

'Yes,' she said honestly, but was unable to resist adding, 'That is, once I became used to dealing with executives. A far cry from the usual people your average librarian meets, I assure you.'

He laughed. 'Had to fight them off, did you?'

It was an effort, but she managed to dampen the sudden insistent response she felt. He had always been able to make her laugh. Lightly, her voice very cool, she said, 'Some. The married ones were the worst.'

'Marriage,' he told her, 'is often more like a strait-jacket than the haven we hope it might be.'

There was no cynicism in the gravelly voice, no anger, yet she sensed some extremely powerful emotion. Her gaze lifted, searched the dark, rakish face. Finding it impassive, his eyes almost hidden by the heavy lids, she looked away.

Some instinct impelled her to say awkwardly, 'I—I was sorry to hear that yours didn't work out.'

'Were you?' Now he did look sardonic, those pale

eyes gleaming beneath his lashes. 'You used not to lie, Melissa. It was one of your most attractive traits, that transparent honesty.'

She hated the way his mouth twisted as he spoke. 'Really?' she returned calmly.

'Yes. What shattered your illusions, made you hide behind everyday falsehoods?'

He was needling her, cruelly provoking a reaction, but she had herself well in hand now. The years which had hardened him had given her poise and a sophistication that made it almost easy to hide her emotions.

'I suppose it's just maturity,' she parried, letting her eyes drift slowly over his rawboned features. It wasn't quite so easy to allow a little speculation to colour her dark eyes, or her smile, but she managed to do it, finishing with, 'Who was it who said "Experience is a good teacher, but she sends enormous bills"?'

'A cynic,' Trent returned softly, his eyes watchful. 'Are you a cynic now, Melissa?'

Her shoulders lifted, dismissing the smooth caressing note in his voice. 'Perhaps it was the same person who said that a cynic is a bruised romantic. I'm neither; I'm a realist.'

'Goethe said that if a man destroys the power of illusion, either in himself or in others, Nature punishes him like the harshest tyrant. Have I done that to you?'

'Destroyed my illusions?' Pride lifted her head, curved her mouth in a tantalising little smile. 'No, it wasn't you. My experience with Derek began the process, you continued it, but living in London spurred things on. It happens to all of us, after all. You included.'

His brows lifted slightly as he surveyed her face, those chilling eyes recognising the taunt, and appreciating it. Yet when he spoke it was at a tangent.

'Have there been many men for you? Does the good life pall after a while?'

'No and no,' she said calmly. 'How many would you say was too many? Four? A dozen? A hundred?'

That pirate's smile showed even, very white teeth for a second before the harshly outlined face resumed its usual mocking expression. Pretending to consider, he said, 'I think I can discount a hundred. Even a dozen. That would have given you a new man every three months. Of course, you could be truly liberated and go in for one-night stands. No?' Her head snapped dangerously around. 'Then I'll allow you four, as it came so pat to your lips. A Freudian slip? Good, five has always been my lucky number. I'm not superstitious, but if I were I'd bet consistently on it. It's amazing how often it's shown up in my affairs, and always to my advantage.'

Melly's black brows drew together. 'I don't know what you're babbling about,' she said, a faint note of hauteur hiding her unease.

'I'd have thought it was self-evident.' He drained his coffee, set the mug on to the table beside his chair and smiled, a slow, wolfish, untamed smile that reinforced the searing message of his eyes as they swept her face before sliding with insolent and lingering thoroughness down the length of her body. Wherever they touched they kindled fires.

Stiffly, battling the colour that heated her skin, she countered, 'I must be slow, then, because I don't know what the hell you're getting at. And if you'll excuse me, I am going out shortly.'

She got to her feet, hating to lie, yet suddenly, viciously, attacked by a long-repressed pain.

'I'm sorry, you should have said.' He stood up, not believing her, that contemptuous smile pulling at the corner of his mouth. With arrogant confidence he went on, 'I'll spell it out for you, then.'

Melly had begun to pick up her coffee mug. The statement, and his tone of voice, stopped her. Slowly she straightened, her hands tensing at her sides. She stared at the mug.

'No!' she said harshly.

'I'd hate you to get the wrong idea. I intend to be your fifth lover,' Trent went on as though she hadn't objected. There could be no mistaking the hard determination in his voice.

Somewhere, in some place hidden so deep inside her that she had forgotten its existence, his words struck home. It was like the quick flaring of a star gone nova, a white-hot explosion, more emotional than physical, and yet her body was aching with a strange, slow languor. Slowly her head lifted. What she saw in his face made her step backwards. 'No,' she repeated through lips as bloodless as the rest of her skin. The little syllable cracked in two.

'Yes.' He made no attempt to hide the open desire that blazed with a fierce fire in his expression.

Panic left Melly with a frantically beating heart and a kind of hollow fear which lodged in her stomach. The sudden shift in Trent from amused mockery to determination underlined with sensual menace was unnerving. Her lips trembled, then tightened. The detachment in his eyes was more frightening because with it went that blatantly sexual appraisal.

But most frightening of all was her body's treachery; it throbbed now with a bitter, elemental need that made her desperate with the desire to get rid of him.

'Sorry,' she said, trying very hard to sound sophisticated and confident. 'I subscribe to the belief that blowing on dead embers gets you nothing but a sore throat. Now, are you going, or shall I call——?'

'Who? Big brother is a bit too far away to rescue you.'

'Oh!' Her long fingers clenched into fists. 'Will you please go?' she demanded, all attempts at worldly self-assurance gone.

'Typical woman,' he complained, sounding irritable, of all things.

Melissa's eyes flew to his face as an extremely strong hand picked up one of hers; by the application of a little judicious pressure he forced it open.

'If you're going to make a fist,' Trent explained patiently, 'with the intention of using it, the thumb must sit *outside* your fingers. Like this.'

Bemused, she watched as he refolded her hand into a serviceable fist. She made some slight resistance as he pulled it upwards, but one glinting glance from him and she allowed him to rest the knuckles against the rough-smooth line of his chin.

'Twist your fist from palm upwards to palm downwards just before you hit; it gives you extra force,' he continued. 'And aim for the nose, or the Adam's apple, or the solar plexus.'

Gently, inexorably, he shifted her reluctant fist to each of the places he mentioned, finally holding it still against the hard wall of muscle between his rib cage.

Laughter warmed his voice as he went on, 'But only there if he's not expecting it. If the muscle is tightened, as it is now, a jab doesn't get much in the way of results. The most vulnerable place in a man's body is the best place to go for.'

As if her hand had been burnt Melly jerked it behind her back, colour flooding her face.

Trent broke into laughter, his eyes crinkling with an amusement which failed entirely to hide the glitter in them as he scanned her mutinous, outraged face.

'You're easily shocked,' he taunted. 'I'm not so lacking in subtlety, Melissa. When you touch me it will be because you want to, because the only thought in your mind will be to make yourself as familiar with my body as I intend to be with yours. We will learn to know each other, in every meaning of the word, and the learning will be like nothing you've ever experienced before.'

Words trembled on her tongue, but her lips were trembling too, and she could not say them. Like prisoners her eyes were caught and held by his, blazing crystals in the dark determination of his face.

Trent seemed to realise how she felt. He gave her an odd, twisted smile, and lifted her other hand to his mouth, kissing the knuckle with a grace which should have been affected, but fitted his lean piratical elegance well. Against her skin his lips were warm and dry. Melly shuddered, her whole body suffused with a heat which came from some point central to, yet apart from, her body.

'Yes,' he said softly, as his eyes lingered on her soft parted lips, 'I mean it, Melissa. Come and see me out.'

He kept her hand in his and led her out into the hall. At the door he said teasingly, 'Remember to keep your arm bent if you ever have to punch anyone.'

Melly shook her head, and he grinned and said, 'Just one more thing,' and took her in his arms and kissed her mouth with great tenderness before leaving her.

CHAPTER TWO

How long Melly stood staring at the door after it had closed behind his lithe form she didn't know. After a time she raised her hand and pressed her knuckles to her lips, pushing the soft skin against her teeth while disconnected thoughts swirled about in cloudy disarray inside her head.

He means it. He means to become my lover. My *fifth* lover!

A smile ominously close to a grimace contorted her mouth. *Fifth!* If only he knew!

For her there had been no lovers, not one, not even Derek to whom she had been engaged. She had been content to wait; subconsciously, of course, she had not really wanted him very much for one very obvious reason. All through her engagement to him she had been in love with Trent.

His subsequent betrayal seemed to have frozen the responses of her body. Until today. And then every tiny nerve and cell had leapt into life again, bombarding her brain with impulses and information she didn't dare process.

'The nerve!' she said out loud, wrenching her hand from her mouth as she turned away, intent on whipping up anger to submerge the memory of that moment when Trent's lips had touched hers and she had responded with an exquisite excitement as though she was still an adolescent at the mercy of her body and emotions.

It worked. Within five minutes she was furious with him, furious with herself for not slapping his face, furious with Fate and Coincidence and several other

personifications for so arranging things that Rafe
should have chosen this block of all blocks to lease an
apartment in. Savagely reflecting on the unfortunate
fact that both men had sufficient wealth to afford one
of the extremely expensive suites carried her through
another cup of coffee she didn't want and her
preparations for bed.

Once there, she read the same sentence in her book
about thirty times before switching off the lamp with a
sharp, angry gesture, only to lie with her eyes open,
staring at the ceiling while her treacherous mind
wondered about the plan of the penthouse above and
her ears strained to hear non-existent sounds. It seemed
hours before she dozed off and then it was a restless,
unsatisfactory sleep with vivid dreams to disturb her.

How long the bell had been ringing before it
impinged she didn't know. Startled, her head thick, she
groped for the telephone, but after a scrambled few
seconds realised that someone was leaning on the door
bell.

At the door she switched on the communications
device and asked, 'Who is it?'

'Trent,' came back the brisk answer. 'I left my
briefcase behind and I need it. I put it beside the
bookshelf.'

Sure enough, there it was. Slowly she picked it up. It
was leather, not new, but with that indefinable scent,
most pleasing.

When the door swung open he straightened up from
the wall, removing his hands from his pockets as he
eyed her with a quizzical smile.

He had changed from the formal business suit to grey
trousers and shirt and a thin dark red jersey that picked
up the glowing highlights in his hair.

'Thank you,' he said calmly, taking the briefcase
from her. 'I'm sorry I woke you.' There was a moment
of silence before he continued with smooth effrontery,

'You look very young, all tousled and slightly damp behind the ears.'

An angry swathe of colour heated Melly's high cheekbones; she found herself clutching her cotton dressing-gown across her breasts. A gleam of some unknowable emotion flared in his eyes, but when she backed a hasty step away it was extinguished by his heavy lids and he gave that twisted smile she hated.

'No, you're quite safe tonight,' he said, leaving her in no doubt of his meaning as his eyes roved boldly over her. 'I've waited four years for you, a few more weeks won't strain me too much. I don't go in for rape scenes.'

She opened her mouth in indignation and his head swooped, his mouth covered hers in a kiss which was bold and seeking and flagrantly sensual. His free arm came across her back, clamping her to the hard, taut refuge of his body. Then she was free and he was laughing, although he breathed heavily.

'Goodnight, sweet nymph,' he said mockingly. 'I have your counterpart gracing my pool.'

Bitterly she flung back, 'And the satyr, too?'

Those black straight brows lifted. 'Well, the description in the catalogue states that he's a faun. But yes, now that you mention it, he eyes my pretty nymph with an exceedingly lustful stare.'

Melly slammed the door shut to the sound of his laughter, shaking her head to clear it while her heart beat heavily in her ears.

After that, sleep fled entirely. She spent most of what was left of the night trying to woo it while her tired brain went lovingly, sadly, over the circumstances of their first meeting.

She had been almost twenty and Trent had been eight years older, already something of a celebrity for his business acumen in the electronics industry. They had met at a friend's place and she had been intrigued and fascinated by him, so much so that it took all of her considerable willpower to keep her mind on her university course.

When he asked her out she had been excited and hopeful, enjoying his company immensely, for he had the ability to make her forget that rumour made him a sophisticated and rather dangerous man.

Had she fallen in love with him then? Even now she didn't know. Probably not; she had been an immature girl caught in the toils of her first strong bout of sexual attraction. That she had liked and respected him as well only made it more enchanting.

It was a wonder she had managed to sit her exams, she thought wryly, let alone pass them well. When the university year ended she should have gone home to Te Puriri, but she had lingered, falling deeper and deeper beneath his spell, until Rafe came down.

And told her that all those years before it was Trent who had persuaded Jennet into an affair which had ended her marriage to Derek, who had been Trent's cousin. Melly could still remember her horror, the sensation that something very precious had been befouled. She had always liked Derek and often wondered why her half-sister had fled to Australia after only eight months of marriage to him, but no one had ever told her.

Had she been older, more mature, she would have faced Trent with the reason for her rejection, but she had behaved badly, running back to the sanctuary of Te Puriri. And there had been Derek, next door, charming, light-hearted, and very appreciative of the older Melly.

What had she felt for the man she became briefly engaged to? Not love, she thought, frowning. Nothing but hurt pride and anger and jealousy on both sides had produced that engagement. Unconsciously Melly had used Derek to anaesthetise her feelings for Trent. The memory of her behaviour still had the power to make her feel cheap, a little shoddy.

Afterwards she had been chastened, afraid of the results of her thoughtlessness. And with immense patience Trent had set out to coax her back into his arms. Before her mother had borne her off to her home in the South of France for a holiday, Melly had been in love. All the clichés had applied, she thought now with a cynical little smile. Head over heels, fathoms deep—she had been lost in him. It was reciprocated, too. They had talked of marriage, even set a tentative date.

So when it had come, the letter in which he rejected her, the cold ugly words had killed something in her, leaving her open to her mother's cynical, well-meaning advice.

'Everyone has to have their heart broken once,' Diana had said, almost cheerfully. 'It's a rite of passage.'

Melly had turned, biting her lip, to look at her mother's exquisite blonde beauty. 'Even you?'

'Even me. It taught me never to leave myself open to that kind of pain again.'

'And are you happy?'

Diana had laughed. 'A lot happier than if I'd married him,' she said complacently. 'Believe me, Melly, love lasts for a year, maybe two. After that it passes.'

Melly had not agreed, and still didn't entirely. The weeks she had just spent at Te Puriri with Rafe and Jennet had convinced her that for some lucky people love remained, glowing and tender and fierce. Perhaps they were unique. She had deliberately embraced Diana's outlook, finding in it some kind of hope, and sure enough, after a year the pain had almost gone. She had thought that incandescent attraction, that elemental call of male to female had died with it. Until tonight.

'No,' she said through clenched teeth, anger spiking the word. No, not again, not ever again. She was not going to put herself in his power again. Armed with her knowledge of the quick opportunism which was the flaw in his character, she was strong enough to resist his lust.

Her mind drifted, recalling the strange tenderness he showed occasionally, the gentle care with which he had treated her after the débâcle of her engagement. Jennet, she knew, thought there was a reason other than ambition and the desire for power which had led Trent to marry Cathy Durrant, but to Jennet he was the saviour who had carried her off from an intolerable marriage after Derek had so crushed her spirit that she was incapable of freeing herself.

Trent Addison was strong, ruthless; not a man to be forced into anything. His buccaneering instincts went deeper than the surface. He was a complicated, subtle personality, greed and kindness intermingled, cruelty and gentleness woven together in the fabric of his character. Melly knew that she would ignore or underrate him at her peril.

In her own way Melly could be just as ruthless. It showed now in the way she subdued the flickering glow of excitement which had been aroused by his blatant announcement of his intentions. In exactly the same way she had quenched the savage jealousy which the vision of Cathy in his arms had caused, with determination and an obstinate refusal to admit that she cared.

But oh, it was cruel of Fate to send him to the very place where she lived!

She was turning over the possibility of moving out when eventually she fell into a deep sleep. If she dreamed of a tall, enigmatic man, she wasn't aware of it when she awoke the next morning.

What she was aware of was a not unpleasant tension, an edge to her perceptions which made her vividly aware of everything, the pale blue of the sky, the brisk wind that tousled the trees in the gardens below, the extra crispness to the air.

It was a pleasant morning, infinitely relaxing after the tense hours last night. After lunch Melly changed into a light linen dress which made the most of her long lovely legs and set out to look up an old school friend who lived not too far away.

They had a riotous afternoon and Melly stayed to dinner, the friend's husband driving her home just before eleven. As the car swung into the street her eyes flicked up, registered the lights in the penthouse and then fell to the tense hands in her lap.

'Shall I come up with you?'

Smiling, she shook her head. 'No. The security is very tight. I'm perfectly safe.'

But he was the chivalrous sort. 'Won't take a moment, and Sara would want me to make sure you got home safely.'

So he did, leaving her at the door with a smile and a wink. Yawning, pleasantly tired, Melly slit open the envelope of a letter from her mother. It read just like Diana, self-centred, shallow yet amusing.

'No man's worth it,' she had told Melly in the days when it had seemed that she was sinking into a miserable kind of self-pity. 'Not a single one, so stop thinking life's passed you by. Life is a compromise. It's no big deal. One day the pain will be gone.'

She had been right there. The pain of loving a man who let his ambition override his love had faded almost into nothingness.

Strange, Melly thought as she put the letter down, that she had never doubted his love. Even after her shocked reading of the letter in which he renounced her she knew he had loved her, but when he saw the chance of acquiring real power without grinding effort he had whistled his love down the wind. Which made his betrayal all the greater.

Now all that was left was the leaping wildfire that was passion. Romantic love, fire and ice, the depths of hell and the heights of rapture, that intensity of liking and respect and desire, that had fled with the empty years.

Yet they were still linked, the bonds between them as strong as—as lust. This unbearable restlessness was a symptom of her body's readiness for a lover; well, she thought, smiling a cold little smile, I'll exercise it away.

But after a bath she was still restless, and the spectre of another sleepless night kept her tossing in the bed.

Willpower was no use. Sleep couldn't be forced, it had to be wooed, but when she tried relaxing, clearing her mind, sleep was too coy to come.

It was intensely quiet. The soundproofing was excellent, she thought sourly, trying hard to freeze that part of her brain that wondered why the penthouse had lights on in every room. Perhaps he was having a party . . .

She *had* to get some sleep. Tomorrow was the first day of her new job and if she didn't sleep she'd look like death. One of the penalties of having a skin that clear warm olive colour was that it turned horribly sallow when she was tired or off-colour. And black eyes needed a sparkle to prevent them from looking flat and opaque. Nobody looked less efficient than a tall woman with curls that sagged limply about a drawn face.

'Sleep, damn you!' she told herself bitterly.

Eventually, of course, she did, subsiding into the heavy slumber which makes the alarm an intolerable, frightening intrusion. Totally disorientated, Melly lay supine for some minutes before staggering with a groan to the shower. It helped to revive her, as did the pot of yoghurt and the gold-fruit she ate for breakfast, but it was the second cup of tea that made her feel almost human.

It was a brilliant day, blue-skied and glowing with just enough breeze to temper the humid heat. Melly found herself humming as she pulled on the white

A-line pullover dress she had decided to wear. Pleats from the low waist swung briskly about her slender legs and when the vee-necked jacket with its double-breasted fastening at hip level was in place she was relaxed enough to smile. The whole outfit had a faintly fifties air, but it suited her tall ripeness and it was a fresh counterpoint to the day. The white made her look a little sallow; she had just put on blusher and lipstick when the doorbell rang.

'Oh—hell!' she complained crossly to her reflection. Of all the mornings to have an unexpected visitor! At least she had the perfect reason for getting rid of whoever it was.

But the voice on the entry-phone was Trent's, decisive and crisp and obviously not expecting rejection or dismissal.

'Come on,' it said. 'You're going to be late if you waste too much time.'

'I—*what*?'

'Open the damned door!'

Compelled by the hard authority of his command, she did just that, her face reflecting her astonishment even as her body tightened against the threat his dark magnetism represented. Ice-grey eyes swept over her in one comprehensive glance.

'Very elegant,' he drawled, as he came in through the door. 'Get your bag, there's a good girl, and we'll be off.'

Recovering quickly, Melly stopped backing away to point out coldly, 'I'm almost ready to leave for work.'

'I'm ready.' He grinned. 'Hurry up and I'll take you.'

'You don't know——'

'Of course I do.'

It didn't take the amused derision in his voice to tell her, she had known ever since she heard his voice.

Her mouth tightened. 'Was it a put-up job?'

'Don't be a fool,' he said calmly. 'I'm a businessman,

Melissa, with jobs hanging on each decision I make. You had the best qualifications, you were hired before I even saw your name. Now go and get your bag, I don't like being late.'

'I can't turn up with you.'

'Why not?' Apparently bored with waiting, he turned her around. One hand in the small of her back propelled her gently, inexorably, across the room. Reasonably he continued, 'I made no secret of the fact that I know you. Why should I?'

'That's different,' she almost wailed, her poise deserting her. 'Knowing you is one thing, arriving with you in your car on the first day is another, and you damned well know it!'

'Don't swear, I don't like it.'

'Tough!' she retorted belligerently.

His laughter was low with an edge to it.

'Yes, I remember that temper. You should have learned to control it by now.'

From between gritted teeth she said, 'Oh, if I'd realised that it was important to you, no doubt I'd have done so.'

Trent stopped in mid-stride, the hand which had been urging her on fastening on to her upper arm to jerk her around to face him. Melly stared at him, her defiant expression assumed hastily to hide a strange cold fear. He was smiling. That was, his mouth was stretched into the configuration of a smile, but there was no amusement in his expression, nothing but a cold purposefulness. The pale gaze was empty of all emotion except for a frozen threat.

In that moment Melly knew what real fear was.

Then his lashes fell and the smile relaxed into mockery, as if that moment of heart-chilling menace had never happened.

Yet there was a hint of it in the abrasive tone in which he said, 'You know now, Melissa.'

'I don't consider it important—or necessary—to pander to your whims.' She spoke through lips stiff with pride, her head held high on a neck that ached.

'So reconsider.'

Before she had time to come to terms with that flat command Trent had released her and was saying impatiently, 'Get your bag, for goodness' sake, or you'll have the staff deciding you've a bad influence on me.'

It seemed that she was going to have to accept this particular piece of high-handedness. Haughtily picking up her bag, she cast a last look around the room, then strode for the door, ignoring the man who followed so closely behind that she could feel his nearness prickling her skin.

In the garage beneath the building, he guided her towards a Daimler, dark blue and opulently severe, putting her into the front passenger's seat with a kind of abstracted courtesy that didn't appease her at all. He was shrewd enough to know that since he had forced her into this, it was only sensible to give her a breathing space.

He drove smoothly and well through the rush-hour traffic, not speaking. Melly stared out of the window until, to her irritation, she found herself slanting little glances at the strong incisive line of his profile. He didn't appear to notice until, as the car nosed down towards the parking floor of the building where she had been interviewed, he said blandly,

'I have no intention of seducing you in the car, so you can stop sliding those terrified little glances my way.'

Which left her with nothing to say. She satisfied herself with a fiery stare, direct this time, and was made even more angry by the taunting smile with which he met it.

An hour later she was reflecting cynically that arriving with the boss certainly smoothed out certain aspects of working life. If she hadn't been so angry she would probably have been amused at everyone's startled acknowledgment. Trent delivered her to Personnel, treating her as if she was the younger sister of an old friend. She was the only one who saw the unholy amusement in his eyes before he left her.

Gloomily accepting that within half an hour rumours, wild and creative, would reach the furthermost regions of the building, Melly was introduced to the girl who had been trying to keep things in order; by lunchtime she acknowledged that she was going to be fully extended in this job.

'I did my best,' Susan Field told her, 'but my strong point is filing, not being a librarian, and the stuff just keeps pouring in!'

Well aware that she was going to need to be careful, Melly grinned. 'Nobody can do better than their best, so my big brother informs me. You've given me a good base to work on.'

Susan relaxed, eyeing Melly inquisitively. 'This big brother . . . does he look like you?'

'He does, but he's much married.'

'Oh well, I suppose that leaves me free to join the madding crowd and pursue our dynamic boss.' Susan sighed dramatically, but the blue eyes were speculative as they scanned Melly's face.

'And are you having any success?' The question came with a dry undernote Melly couldn't hide. Susan Field was an extremely attractive girl with skilfully lightened hair and the kind of alluring smile that drew appreciative masculine eyes.

'Alas, no, the man never even sees me, however hard I try. I believe he's a friend of yours.'

'He went to school with my brother,' Melly told her cheerfully. 'I've known him for years.'

How easy it was to lie by omission, to gaze serenely at Susan, to let the words glide from her lips like smooth truths. And how small she felt as Susan nodded, accepting the lie, her speculative gaze touching on Melly's expensively shod feet, the spare, chic lines of her dress, the patrician bones of her face. Melly realised that she was now slotted into place; not Trent's girl-friend, but a member of his social circle.

'A very useful big brother,' Susan said wryly. 'Wish I had a couple with friends like that. On second thoughts though, I wouldn't mind if our gorgeous Mr Addison just looked my way. Unfortunately, rumour has it that he's not at all that keen on us ladies.' Susan was clearly a gossip, but she knew when to stop. 'Pity,' she finished lightly. 'Well, I'll leave you to it. If you want any help, give me a yell.'

By half-past four Melly was feeling the full effects of two nights without much sleep. A message from Trent's correct and intensely curious secretary, informing her that she was to come up to his office, didn't improve her temper, but she decided to obey it. He was, she admitted reluctantly, quite capable of doing something embarrassing if she ignored him and his peremptory message.

When she arrived at the suite of rooms he occupied she was met by the secretary, who was middle-aged and married, a tall, plump woman with shrewd, rather hard eyes and a surprisingly warm smile. She sat Melly down with a magazine and a cup of coffee before telling her that Mr Addison would be ready very soon, then she retired through an inner door.

Ten minutes later, exactly two minutes after Mrs Maddren had left, Melly heard the door to Trent's office open and lifted eyes in which resentment was frosted with disdain. They met his, cold and glinting with sardonic appreciation. 'Ready?' Trent asked. 'Let's go, then.'

Melly had to bite her lip to keep the hot rejoinder back, but she did it, even though she could feel the amusement emanating from him. All the way down in the lift she kept her eyes fixed on to the floor, deciding that she would buy herself a car as soon as she possibly could. Even a second-hand one would deplete her bank balance alarmingly, but when the next quarter's cheque came in she would be able to sell it for a new one.

'You will have,' Trent remarked quietly as he opened the door for her, 'better things to spend your money on.'

With incredulous eyes she watched as he walked around the front of the car. How had he known? But then they had always been able to communicate without words. Once she had thought it revealed how perfect they were for each other.

As he got in he gave her that raffish disturbing grin, long lean hands fastening the seat-belt with the kind of deft efficiency which was a hallmark of the man.

'Now I should smile omnisciently and let you wonder just how I knew what you were thinking,' he said as the engine fired. 'A little healthy awe would be appreciated. However, just to prove to you how open and trustworthy I am, I'll tell you how I knew. As we walked over from the lift you eyed every car we passed with a thoughtful look, obviously weighing them up, with an especially keen assessment of the smaller ones. It didn't take a mind-reader to work out what was going on inside your head.'

The sun dazzled her eyes, making her blink, providing her with the perfect excuse for putting on dark glasses.

As the big car wove through the slackening traffic she said stiffly, 'I hate it when you make me seem so—so transparent.'

'Do you?' The pause hummed with unsaid words. Rather drily he continued, 'And I suppose you hate the fact that it's your honesty which I admire.'

'On the principle of admiring the things we haven't

got?' she asked, masking the taunt with a cool politeness.

His mouth hardened, then curved into a sardonic smile. 'Perhaps. Where would you like to go for dinner?'

'I'm not—Trent, I won't let you do this to me! I don't want to go out to dinner with you, or go to work with you or——'

'Sleep with me,' he interpolated neatly.

'—have anything to do . . . *What* did you say?'

'Guess.'

Colour poured into the smooth clarity of her skin in a great wave of heat as her head jerked around. The thin lips were still smiling, the arrogant profile harsh against the brilliant light outside.

Poor Melly's mouth hung open for several feeble seconds; she had to will herself to close it.

'I am not going to put up with this—this harassment,' she said in a tight, angry voice.

'Then the sooner you give me what I want, the sooner this harassment will be over.'

'I do not want to have an affair with you.' She spoke in a hard, gritty voice, each word snapping between lips tense with anger and strain.

His brows lifted and he slanted her a quick, mischievous glance, subtly mocking her outrage. 'Of course you do,' he said soothingly. 'You know, you have very little imagination. It could give you the perfect revenge. Think of how much fun you'll have subjugating me and then walking off, leaving me desolate.'

'You don't know the meaning of the word,' she retorted, sternly repressing some crazy part of her brain which would have liked to dwell on the idea.

'Teach me, then.'

Just for a moment, for a dangerous few seconds, Melly toyed with the idea, but the elemental masculine confidence he didn't know he had and couldn't hide soon put an end to that. He was seducing her, tempting her to use weapons of his choosing in a battle in which he was certain that he would be the victor.

'Don't be an idiot,' she said quickly, scornfully, so that he wouldn't know just how much she wanted to be tempted. 'Anyway, I'm going out with someone else tonight.'

'You really must stop this lying. You're far too conscientious to have decided to go out on the night after your first day working. I'll bet you've decided to go for a run, take a long bath and then to to bed early so that you'll be relaxed and refreshed tomorrow morning.'

Almost she ground her teeth! Then grabbing rather desperately at her usual smooth cloak of self-control, she said, 'And that is exactly what I intend to do.'

'After you've had dinner,' he told her with cheerful lack of interest in her anger. Hammering home the point, he finished, 'With me.'

'*I do not want* to have dinner with you!'

'Tough.'

Melly had to clasp her hands together in her lap to stop herself from hitting him, not in the least helped by his sympathetic sideways grin, or the hand that covered hers for a second.

'Indulge me in this,' he said softly as the car turned into the immaculate grounds of the apartment block.

His gentleness breached a gap in the defences that his hard assurance had failed to penetrate. She swallowed, unwilling eyes noting the deep lines engraved in the strong privateer's face. She was not the only one who was tired.

To hide the sudden surge of tenderness she asked acidly, 'Don't you enjoy being a tycoon as much as you thought you would, Trent?'

The engine switched off. In the cavernous garage he

turned to her, his eyes as clear as quartz, as hard, as sharp.

'Enjoy? Yes, I suppose I enjoy it. It's hard work, and I get tired, but it's nothing like it was at first. I've managed to pull things together. I have a good team around me, I delegate as much as possible.'

Interested against her will, she ventured, 'Had Sir Peter left it in such a mess, then?'

The hard eyes closed, then flicked open. 'I'm afraid so. He stayed on long after he should. If he'd had a son—but Cathy's father was killed when she was only two.' The wide shoulders lifted in a slight shrug. 'I think Sir Peter began to lose interest then.'

He was watching her closely, no doubt to see how the mention of his ex-wife's name affected her. It still hurt, but it was the casual way he spoke it, as though Cathy Durrant had meant nothing to him. Not a flicker of emotion for the woman who had shared his bed and his name, nothing, not anger or pain or affection or irritation.

Melly went cold. Her skin tightened over flesh and bones held rigid in a cast of despair. If Trent had told her word by word he could not have made it plainer that that brief marriage had been one of expediency only. Once he had acquired control of Sir Peter's holdings, it had been severed as cruelly and swiftly as a knife thrust in the dark.

And this was the man she had learned to love, had wept for and ached for and yearned for in an agony of disillusion, had allowed her life to be altered by! For the past years had been marked by her refusal to allow any man to get close to her. A coward, she had been afraid of the possibility of pain.

Now, transfixed, she realised how futile it had been. He was simply not worth it. He was not even ashamed of what he had done; the dark face was quizzical, almost amused, the narrowed eyes clear as they searched hers.

Looking for what? Weakness? An admission that she was still powerfully attracted to his rangy virile masculinity? Because that was true, too. Even now she could feel the slow elemental beat of her blood through her body speeding and quickening into life impulses and sensations she had long repressed. Her lashes quivered, then lifted. She knew that she was being willed to do something, say something ... But she firmed her mouth and looked away, refusing him whatever it was that he wanted.

'Let's go,' he said harshly, as if she had disappointed him; the hand at her elbow was almost painful, urging her into the lift.

At the ground floor it stopped and a woman Melly didn't know got in. Young, and beautiful in a blonde, ethereal way, she gave a perfunctory smile to Melly and a much warmer one to Trent who, Melly was furious to see, returned it with an appreciation that made the intruder bridle slightly, even while she sent him a complicated beckoning look from beneath her lashes.

Almost certainly dyed, Melly thought waspishly; one of the advantages of being dark was the thick, black lashes that sheltered her eyes. And that hair was too even in colour to be natural. Did she have to be so *flagrant* in her scrutiny? Trent might pretend not to notice the appraisal he was getting, but the corner of his mouth quirked and when he looked over the intruder's head to meet Melly's stare there was wicked laughter in his eyes. She rejected it with contempt.

It died; the heavy lids came down and hid whatever he was feeling. When, after a final seductive smile, the woman got off, Trent observed, apparently idly,

'What a prig you are, Melissa.'

Just that, but the scorn in his voice made her prickle with resentment.

'If that's so,' she returned in her most clipped voice, 'why don't you look somewhere else for a companion at dinner? After all, a *prig* is hardly likely to be amusing company.'

'Possibly not, but we'll keep to the original arrangement. I don't want to be entertained.'

The lift bell gave its soft 'ting' and the lift slowed to a halt, the doors whispering apart. Trent's hand at her elbow urged Melly into a large vestibule; his voice was soft as he said, 'No, not entertained. Stirred, excited, stimulated, even aroused; but amusement is not what I had in mind.'

It must be the day for clarifying things, Melly thought furiously as her mind processed that remark. Clearly he was making certain she didn't have any illusions about his plans for her. No suggestion of love or marriage, nothing so banal. He wanted nothing from her but a sating of the physical effect her lithe young body had on him. Passion, lust, desire, all of the words that language finds to camouflage the basic primitive urge to mate. All that he felt for her, all that was left of the tender love they had once shared.

CHAPTER THREE

His apartment was beautiful, not the stark, ultra-modern place she had been subconsciously expecting, but a restful sweep of floor, carpet and travertine marble of identical colour, superb contemporary Italian sofas and chairs and an original unstylised combination of paintings and sculpture and plants. Like Jennet's rooms on the floor below it bore the stamp of its owner, distinctive, the result of a perfect marriage between interior decorator and a cultivated, definite mind.

'I'm glad you like it,' Trent said softly. 'You look at home here.'

'Who wouldn't?' she exclaimed, lifting impressed eyes. 'It's—beautiful, as I'm sure you must have been told a hundred times.'

'Not often.' He answered her look of surprise with a twisted smile. 'I appreciate my privacy, Melissa. Few people get invited here.'

For some reason she didn't make the smart remark which leapt to her tongue. Angry though she was, some instinct kept her quiet. Instead she looked at a tapestry on the wall, a magnificent thing of tension and splendour, baroque in style with its melodramatic use of highlights and shadows. It was a scene of trees and animals and birds with a distinct resemblance to Rubens' paintings.

'It's a *verdure*,' said Trent, following her line of sight.

'It's beautiful.' And rather violently expensive, she realised. Te Puriri had been built and furnished in an Italianate style, and there were several tapestries on its walls, but none, she realised, as fine as this.

'Would you like a drink?' he asked.

She shook her head, turning away from the lovely thing. 'No, thanks, I'd like a shower and a change of clothes.'

'In ten minutes I'll take you down to your place. In the meantime, step out into the garden and look at the view.'

The garden was amazing, a rooftop arbour with a pool and plants in beds, not tubs. They had been carefully chosen to cope with the wind and the unobstructed sun, tough South African proteas, hardy Australian shrubs, a few native New Zealand trees to give green comfort to the eye. And yes, there was the nymph, a smoothly sensual bronze, eyed with fervent pleasure by a satyr which had to be Roman.

Like his apartment, the garden was completely, distinctly Trent Addison's.

Melly eyed the dark waters in the pool with some wistfulness. It was still hot, and she was tired and slightly sticky. Slowly, wondering just how she could cope with a situation which seemed to have blown up in her face, she paced the length of the garden, stopping to admire the view over the suburbs and on across the waters of the Waitemata harbour, island-sprinkled, gleaming in the light of the dipping sun.

Could she lead him on, then fling his desire in his teeth as he had done with her love?

The answer has to be no. *Never*. Her brain told her, her emotions warned her, even her body shouted its fear with suddenly cold skin and a momentary clenching of every muscle. Only a fool would challenge Trent. Beneath that charming, worldly surface there was the pirate, ruthless with a single-minded determination, cruel, heartless enough to sacrifice his love for material advantages.

Her feet had led her to an arbour hung about with jasmine, footed with great pots of hippeastrums. Enormous stalks held high the huge flower buds. Still green, they were almost ready to split to reveal the huge trumpets so miraculously hidden within. In a week, ten days perhaps, this would be like a voluptuary's heaven, with the heavy scent of the jasmine and the exotic scarlet and crimson of the flowers at their feet.

Melly sat down on the little seat, staring at the pale gold of her linked hands against her white dress. Three years was a long time to hang on to the ravishment of romance. She had worked hard to kill the love she had known, and had succeeded. Had Trent done the same? Almost certainly. He was too cynical to have cherished the flame for that time when he had so willingly betrayed it. Slowly, heavily, her head lifted, the black curls clinging to her temples and forehead. He was watching her, his expression forbidding and remote as though he was gazing at something achingly unattainable.

And into Melly's mind there came an unbidden memory from the past, from the days when she had been engaged to Derek. She had walked on to Rafe and Jennet as they kissed beside the pool at Te Puriri and although they had not then admitted their love to each other she had realised that they were two halves of one whole. How angry she had been! And at the back of that anger had been a deep tearing envy, for she had never known such passion.

Much later, in Trent's arms, she had thought it possible, although he had been tender rather than displaying the savage erotic power she had glimpsed that day at Te Puriri. But now, she thought as her heart beat unevenly, now that he thought her experienced and no longer a virgin, how would he kiss her? How would he love her now?

He was coming towards her, moving with the easy grace and balance that marked him out, lithe, powerful, his determination enveloping him like an aura. Melly sat quietly waiting, while the blood rushed through her veins in a heated turmoil.

'Tired?' he asked, the word a caress as he held his hand out.

She took it and he pulled her into his arms, holding her a moment against his lean strength. Then he released her and slid an arm over her shoulders, walking her sedately back towards the house.

'A little. The first day at a new job is bound to be exhausting.'

Little shivers of delight were running through her body. Trent's arm was heavy; she could feel his warmth through the light silk of his shirt. A faint masculine scent excited her; every nerve and fibre was taut, transmitting urgent messages to her brain.

'Trent?'

'Mmm?'

She stopped, looking up at him with wary eyes. 'If I asked you to leave me alone, would you?'

The strong framework of his face seemed to harden. Heavy lashes swept down to narrow his gaze into a weapon, stabbing, painful as it swept her face. At last he shook his head.

'Good try, Melissa, but no.'

'Why?'

The straight dark brows lifted, giving him a mocking, almost derisive air. 'Because I want you,' he told her with cool insolence. Melly's mouth opened, but before she could utter her protest he finished, 'And because you want me, my heart. If you didn't you wouldn't have been frightened into making that betraying little plea.'

'Oh, I want you.' Incurably honest, she didn't even try to prevent the harsh words. Her mouth tightened, lending her a momentary severity. 'But I can't—I *will not* leap hotfoot into bed with you.'

The deliberate vulgarity made him laugh softly as he tightened his arm. She was pulled against him so fiercely that her warm curves melded into the hard contours of his body.

'I think you're asking to be wooed,' he said into her hair. 'Do you really believe that I'm so crass as to expect nothing more than a quick roll in the hay? I'm almost shattered. You have a very low opinion of me. Of course I intend to court you.' His hand slid up her throat, the thumb insistently pushing her chin up so that her flushed face was exposed to the glitter of his gaze.

Her eyes dilated as his face approached hers, his breath sweet and warm on the sensitive skin. 'Like this,' he said huskily, kissing her eyes closed, 'and this,' as his mouth touched her cheekbones and the soft lobes of her ears, 'and this . . .'

Bemused, her body awash with tides of pleasure, Melly made an indeterminate noise which sounded treacherously close to a plea.

'Soon,' he promised on an indrawn breath, 'oh, soon, Melissa, just as soon as you learn to trust me.'

The words didn't register, how could they? Her brain was too busy coping with the erotic sensations engendered by his mouth and that husky, thickened voice and the startling desperate novelty of being so close to him that she could feel every bone, every muscles and sinew as if they were her own.

I don't want this, her brain shouted, but although her lips moved no sounds emerged.

His mouth touched hers, kissing both outer corners, the soft bow, the full lower lip, tiny, taunting kisses which excited but didn't satisfy the hunger building inside her. She felt drunk, fumes of desire clouding her brain so that she thought only with her body, her skin prickling with heat, her heart thundering. It was difficult to hear anything beyond his harsh breathing and a series of small sounds which had to come from her throat.

Yet he was gentle, as restrained as he had always been, treating her tenderly like the child he had first fallen in love with. Well, years had passed since then, and she was more experienced. Oh, she'd never felt anything like this torment of lust, she had never been tempted to surrender her virginity, but she had been kissed by men who were trying to arouse her, and she wanted that now, her whole body screaming for assuagement of this tempest of sensation.

Trent's arms were tense across her back, but he continued those torturing little kisses, ignoring her silent pleas for more. A kind of anger, joined with the passion he had roused, licked through her veins like a flashfire, and she moved deliberately, thrusting suggestively with her hips against his hard indifference. Her hands left his shoulders, slid into the dark mahogany of his hair and pulled his head down. Careless of any consequences she began to kiss him back, the same avid little kisses across the thin mouth, wanting only to rouse the tiger she knew crouched hidden in his personality.

For long seconds she thought she had failed. The heat in her began to congeal into shame and a kind of panic until with a groan that sounded as though it had been ripped from him, his mouth came savagely down on hers, forcing it open in a kiss that transcended everything she had ever experienced before.

She responded with a fiercely primitive passion, offering all that was female in her to his overwhelming masculinity, her body tightly wound, shivering with anticipation when his hand slid down her spine, pressing her against him so that she realised just what she had invoked with her impetuous desire. She should have been frightened; indeed, the real Melly was afraid, but the real Melly had been superseded by this new Melly, a wanton who revelled in the flood of sensation she was experiencing.

Suddenly the brutal pressure of his mouth on hers eased. His breath was hot on her tender lips as he muttered some words which sounded suspiciously like an apology. Slowly, slumbrously, Melly lifted her lashes to reveal a dazed blank stare from pupils dilated so widely that the iris was swallowed entirely by the blackness. In this foggy, hot world of the senses she wondered why he took a sharp, painful breath.

'Melly,' he said raggedly. 'Oh, Melly...'

Her brows drew together. It was difficult, but she sharpened her gaze, trying to focus on the harsh lines and planes of his face, noting almost absently that there was a flush of colour along the high cheekbones and that the grey eyes were ablaze with a fire she had never seen in them before.

Lust, she thought vaguely, and—yes, there was anger there too, and some other emotion which almost looked like pain.

'What's the matter?' Her mouth trembled as she spoke and her lips were dry so that she had to dampen them with her tongue.

An odd, singing sensation thrilled through her nerves as she saw his eyes flicker, become fixed on the tantalising slide of her tongue along the gentle curves. She smiled, a blindly promising smile as old as the first temptress, and stroked her palms across the slightly rough skin of his cheeks and moved her body against his in the smallest, most explicit of movements.

His groan was music, the quick, violent demand of his mouth bliss, the surge of savage response in her body bewildering, yet it incited her to surrender in the most basic of ways, a surrender she signalled with a wordless little murmur of acceptance and the clasping of her hands behind his back so that they were locked together, body perfectly adjusted to body, his mouth burning into the long length of her throat, her rapt face tipped towards the rapidly darkening sky.

She had got beyond the stage of expectation. She really didn't know what was going to happen next;

worse, she didn't care. His arousal was patent, everything about the leashed urgency of his embrace shouted his desire. If she had been able to struggle free from the miasma of passion that clouded her brain she would have been afraid of this unusual laxness in her, but she didn't, couldn't think, her body was set on overdrive and that was just what it was doing.

As his mouth moved deliberately to the strong line of her jaw her body sang in anticipation, waiting expectantly for the next step. It had happened to her before, the slow slide of the hand to her breast, the tentative movement of fingers; always before she had stopped things right there, moved out of the embrace with a graceful technique refined over quite a few such encounters. But this time she was not going to avoid it. This time she wanted to know just how it would feel to have Trent cup her breast in that lean dark hand, stroke the rounded smoothness as if the feel of it was exciting . . .

And then he straightened up and put her very firmly from him and gave a strange, twisted movement of his lips which might have been meant to be a smile.

And he said unevenly, 'No.'

It was like that first rejection all over again, only that had been contained in cold hard words on a piece of paper and this was real, he was standing so close that he filled her eyes, she could not free her nostrils of the scent of him, she was cold and dragging with a burning ache that seemed centralised in the base of her stomach.

'What?' she said idiotically, because she knew what he meant.

That smile relaxed slightly. To reinforce his statement the dark head sketched a quick headshake. 'No,' he said almost calmly, that give-away breathing beginning to regularise now.

Melly felt cold. Her skin tightened with a shiver. 'Then what was that all about?' she asked, hating him.

'Didn't you hear what I said before we kissed?' When she stared blankly at him he smiled and repeated words she recognised, although she was sure she hadn't heard them before. 'I told you that trust comes first. I'm not going to take you until you trust me.'

It was like being hit in the face with a handful of ice. From somewhere she managed to produce a mirthless smile that stretched her sore mouth.

'You must be joking,' she told him tritely, turning her head away so that those pale eyes couldn't probe past her expression to the emotions beneath.

'Never more serious, I promise you.'

Melly bit her lip, grimaced at the pain and tried to think. At last, angry because her voice wobbled, she said, 'You knew what you were doing when you married Miss Durrant. Can you give me one good reason why I should trust you ever again?'

'Only that you love me.'

She shook her head jerkily to clear the buzzing in her ears. 'On the analogy of *Love suffers long*?' she taunted. 'Sorry, I don't agree. I don't love you, I don't trust you. All that's left is—whatever you like to call whatever it is that caused that last little explosion. Lust.'

The dark brows lifted with quelling hauteur. 'Call it lust if you like, you can't degrade passion so easily. On the day that you admit that you love me I'll show you exactly what it is that made your response so wanton a few minutes ago.'

Black curls swirled as she flung away from him, her chin held pugnaciously high. 'You've let your conquests go to your head, I'm afraid,' she told him in a glacial voice. 'I'm sorry if it panders to your monstrous egoism to believe that I've spent these last years yearning for something only you can give me, but the reality is quite different. I got over you quite easily, just as I got over Derek, just as I'll get over any other man I'm stupid enough to allow too close to me. I don't love you. I want you, which is quite different.'

'Is it?' Trent smiled grimly. 'For me, darling girl, the two are inextricably intertwined.'

'Oh, sure.'

He reacted to the scoffing retort with a hand on her shoulder, swinging her around to face him. For a moment grey eyes blazed into black, neither giving quarter, the expression on the woman's smooth face uncannily echoed in the stark contours of the man's face above her.

Then the vicious grip on her shoulder eased, the strong hand slid across her shoulder until his fingertips rested with rather too much emphasis for comfort across the delicate hollows at the base of her throat. As her pulse throbbed against his finger his eyes held hers, and he smiled crookedly.

'Now,' he said in the blandest of tones, 'let's get going. If we can't satisfy one appetite I'd like to satisfy another, and I'm hungry.'

Something in his stance, or that predatory smile, made her nervous. 'I'm not going out to dinner with you,' she said huskily.

'Of course you are.'

That was all, but she turned obediently and walked across the beautiful room, aware that he had once more taken the initiative away.

He waited while she showered and pulled on a straight black skirt with a slit that revealed the sleek golden length of one leg to just below mid-thigh. Over it she wore a red camisole top, the material printed with white leaves. A scarlet belt defined her narrow waist, sandals with high heels and a long rope of beads in the same scarlet allied to a slim clutch bag, lifted the simple little outfit to something special. She had much more opulent dresses in her wardrobe, but she was not, she thought angrily as she coloured a mouth still tender from Trent's onslaught, going to dress up for him.

Still, the little outfit looked good on her. And although he had that infuriating knack of being able to hide his thoughts behind those heavy eyelids of his, she couldn't help an ignoble satisfaction at the appreciation which gleamed in his eyes when he saw her.

'Won't you need a coat?' he asked politely.

'I doubt it. It's humid enough to make me sticky, and being Auckland, it's not likely to cool down much. Anyway, I can't be late.'

His smile matched hers for irony. 'Nor I,' he agreed smoothly. 'Tycoons need a lot of sleep. Running an industrial empire is exhausting.'

Melly had set off for the door, but this stopped her. Almost fearfully she turned her head, her eyes scanning his impassive face. After a moment she said bitterly, 'I don't want to hear about your industrial empire.'

'Sorry,' he said, but he wasn't. He came towards her and took her arm, urging her towards the hall. 'But you will, whenever I want to speak about it. It's there, and I'm not pretending it's not.'

And I suppose I'll have to bear Cathy Durrant's name, Melly thought with fierce scorn, but she didn't have the courage to say that. Instead she said, 'You want too much.'

They had reached the door. Trent looked down at her, the piratical face suddenly almost primitive in its fierceness. 'I want *everything*,' he told her harshly. 'And I'm going to have it. I want what's mine.'

'You forfeited——'

'You belong to me, you always have. I've waited long enough, we've had too many detours along the way, but this time it's going to happen.' He turned her, his strong hands framing her face, his face blazing with a set purpose. 'And I don't just want an affair either, Melly, so forget that. You're going to marry me and give me all that passion you've wasted on others. And more. I'm not going to be content until you confess that you love me.'

Defiance pulled at her features, abraded her voice. 'Then you'll be miserable until the day you die, because that's how long you'll have to wait.'

Black fire glittered in her eyes, anger combining with pain to hide the tears that shimmered over the pupils. His hands trembled and then she was free, staring up into the icy composed mask that was his face.

Through his teeth he said, 'Haven't we wasted enough time? Years and years, all grey, only bearable because there was so much to do that I could push you to the back of my mind——'

'*Don't!*' She could not bear it, could not stand there while he lied—or worse, told her the truth. Abruptly she whirled about, her graceful body tense with outrage. Her teeth began to chatter; she had to press them together until her jaw ached before she could control her voice enough to say, 'Shouldn't we be going?'

It was surrender of a sort, but more bearable than being forced to hear him talk about the results of his betrayal. Because he meant it, there had been a searing intensity in the deep voice which couldn't be misinterpreted.

'Of course,' he said in cool, bland tones, as though he too had been shaken by his momentary lack of self-control.

The restaurant was a small, discreet one on the waterfront at Devonport, the marine suburb across the harbour. It looked out over the waters of the Waitemata Harbour, green and glistening and cool, and served superb seafood.

As she ate fillets of John Dory *en papillote* Melly found herself following Trent's example, speaking in a cool polite voice while the sky darkened outside and family groups walked their dogs along the beach, competing with swimmers and joggers for space.

She drank as sparingly of the excellent wine as he did, refusing to look directly at the dark intent face across the table. Outside, yachts swayed past and she made them an excuse to incline her face sideways, admiring them, asking questions. Once he used to race his own, a lean stripped-down machine built for speed with absolutely no comforts, and only the most basic of conveniences. He had sold it years ago, he told her, but something in his voice dragged her eyes from their fixed gaze and she saw regret in his expression.

Hardening her heart, she said lightly, 'One of the penalties of tycoonery, Trent?'

'Unfortunately, yes.'

She waited until the waiter refilled her glass before continuing maliciously, 'But I'm sure the good outweighs the bad.'

'Are you? What do you know of my world, Melissa?'

'I know that the pursuit of power corrupts just as much as power itself is supposed to.'

His smile was sardonic, a mirthless movement of thin lips. 'I'm afraid you're right,' he said obliquely. 'What do you think would happen if Durrants fell into the wrong hands?'

Her shoulders lifted defensively. One finger pushed along the tablecloth; she felt his eyes on the slender length of it and hastily pulled her hand back and folded it on her lap.

'I don't know. I suppose they'd be taken over by someone else.'

'People would lose jobs,' he said. 'Ultimately, that's the bottom line. No profits, no jobs. Do you know how many people are employed by the companies I control?'

Melly shook her head and he told her, nodding abruptly at her astonishment. 'Of whom you are one,' he said. 'You don't need the money, you're that rare creature, a woman with a private income big enough to keep you comfortably, but most of the people we employ need their jobs badly, especially now when we're going through a recession.'

She understood then what he was trying to do and her mouth tightened.

'And you thought that you were the best man to take on Sir Peter's interests?' she asked, infusing her voice with a delicate contempt.

'They were up for grabs. Hell, Melissa, a year before he died the vultures were squabbling over the disposition of the carcass.'

To still the shaking of her hands she clasped them together beneath the edge of the table, her emotions hidden behind a mask of aloofness as she searched his dark, absorbed features. The skin on her face was stiff, almost painful. 'And did Cathy come as part of the package?'

Beneath his heavy lids his eyes were piercing splinters of crystal. He spoke with his normal arrogant assurance, but she thought he was choosing his words with care. 'I can't discuss her with you. If you want to know anything about our marriage, ask her.'

Momentarily shocked, she stared at him until the rejection registered. Stiffly she replied, 'I have no intention of discussing your marriage with anyone. Ever. I think it's time I went home.'

'Very well then,' said Trent, the uncompromising contours of his face relaxing into less of a withdrawal.

Paradoxically Melly felt a flare of anger at herself. She was so aware of him, so conscious of every tiny thing about him, the many subtle alterations in his expression, the fractional raising of his brows, the muscle that pulled a corner of his mouth inwards, the rugged strength of the bone structure beneath the dark skin—somehow she had absorbed it all. The years had not faded his image; nothing about him was new to her, nothing strange or unwelcome. She knew him as if they had spent long hours together with nothing better for her to do than soak in every detail of him and hide it in her subconscious. And she knew that he was hurting.

It took her a moment to recall that although physically he was closer than her brother, she still knew little of the way his mind worked, and what she did know repelled her. Behind the shuttered features there was a cold, scheming brain capable of betraying love for power.

Harshly, heavily, she said, 'I want to go home now, Trent.'

He looked at her as if he had never seen her before, chilling her with an icy scrutiny. 'Very well,' he repeated, sounding weary, and signalled to the waiter.

They were silent all the way home; Melly sat with her head turned away from him, leaning back into the comfortable seat while her brain warned her not to relax, wondering if he would kiss her when they arrived back.

Unbidden, unwanted, at the thought a spark of sexual excitement glimmered deep within her. It was so unfair that her brain and will should be unable to control the responses of her body.

So Trent was a vital, attractive, sexy man who had had more women than she had had hot dinners! He was also an opportunistic hunter, predatory and without morals as he padded through his particular jungle. He engendered dangerous excitement without conscious effort because that was the sort of man he was, he wore his nature like an aura, crackling with life and energy and that buccaneering, hungry arrogance. He had the strength of his cynicism; no one could surprise him because he expected nothing of anyone. And the reason for that, she thought angrily, was that he wasn't capable of giving anything of himself but his sexual competence and the wealth he had acquired by marrying Cathy Durrant.

Melly forced down her instinctive outcry at her own unfairness. Now was not the time to admit that there was much more to him than that, that he could be kind and tender and amusing, that there was a hidden vein of compassion which ran deep and true through the fabric of his personality. To make such an admission would weaken her, give him a lever in this battle they fought. A cold shiver prickled across her skin as she remembered the husky, grim desire in his voice when he had told her what he wanted.

I want everything, he had said, and she knew he would be satisfied wih nothing less from her. All of it, her love and all the passion she was capable of, her respect and admiration and affection—he wanted her to be totally dependent on him for her happiness.

Why? Because he loved her?

Savagely she repressed the secret little thrill that ran along her nerves. It would be too easy to allow herself to become complacent, to slide back into her habit of loving him.

Remember Cathy Durrant, she told herself bitterly. Sold into a loveless marriage and divorced brutally when her value to him was over.

Yet some treacherous part of her brain told her that he would never treat her so; unless, she countered, another chance for more power came his way. It was unlikely that he would need to jettison his wife to grasp it, but could she ever be happy knowing that he was ruthless enough to sacrifice her if it should become necessary?

There could be only one answer to that.

So lost in her thoughts had she become that the switching off of the engine made her start.

'Home,' Trent said needlessly.

'Home for me is Te Puriri,' she told him in a distant little voice.

There were enough lights in the big basement to reveal the swift, sardonic smile that flashed her way. 'Ah, yes, with big brother. He doesn't like me much. I'm afraid. We meet socially now and then and he looks at me as if I were something rather nasty. I've never been able to work out whether it's because I jilted you or that he still wonders if perhaps I didn't get to know Jennet a little too well when I rescued her from her first husband.'

'That's a beastly thing to say!'

Trent laughed, a soft, jaded sound in the quiet interior of the car. 'True, my darling, but he's an extremely possessive man.'

'He loves Jennet, and he knows as well as I do that she and you didn't—weren't——'

'Lovers?' He supplied the word with a sneering intonation that angered her, but before she could say anything the bland merciless voice continued, 'As it happened, we weren't. But both you and Rafe thought we had been, didn't you?'

Her hands tightened against each other, fingers gripping painfully. Very quietly she said, 'Rafe said—yes, I thought you had been.'

'And the idea disgusted you.'

Fiercely, not caring what such strength of emotion revealed she flung, 'I hated it!'

'Just as you hate the thought of Cathy as my wife.'

But she was once more in control. In glacial tones she returned, 'I no longer care. If I feel anything it's pity for a girl—she was only eighteen, wasn't she?—who was bartered and sold into a commercial marriage. And I despise both of the men who made the bargain.'

'Do you?' Trent turned then, still smiling, although there was nothing but a deadly insolence in his face.

Melly couldn't prevent the way she shrank back. He looked—terrifying, gripped by an intensity of emotion beyond fury. Long fingers worked the clasp of the seatbelt; he leaned over and undid hers, and then his index finger traced a steady intimidating line from the low neck of her camisole to the point of her chin.

'Despise me?' he mused, a note in the gravelly voice

that made her flinch away. 'Sad for you, darling, because despise me or not, hate me or not, you belong to me. You always have. I'd prefer you to accept your fate with an appearance of complaisance; I don't want to hurt you. But if I have to I will, because I don't intend to let you go. You're mine in the most primitive way of all. You're my woman. I'm your man. You know that, otherwise you wouldn't have come home.'

The cold remorseless implacability of his words and expression struck fear into her. Unable to move, she stared as his dark face bent to hers and his mouth touched her mouth.

The briefest of kisses, the slightest of pressures, yet she felt as though she had been branded, mind, body and soul, seared for ever by the force of his purpose.

She had not been conscious of holding her breath, but as his head lifted her breath shivered free of lungs suddenly painful and she slumped back against the seat, shaking.

Trent didn't appear to notice. While he got out of the car she grabbed frantically for the poise to cover her fear and desperation, managing to take several deep, calming breaths. The door opened; his hand helped her out and she stood on legs still absurdly shaky, stiffly keeping her face away from the probing gaze she was beginning to dread.

At the door of her apartment he said politely, 'Good night, Melissa. I'll see you tomorrow morning.'

This broke through the mantle of her emotions. Frowning, her dark eyes watchful in her pale face, she answered, 'I'm quite capable of getting to work myself, thank you.'

He smiled, just as watchfully, with a hint of grim understanding. 'I know, but I want to impress on everyone that you come with me.'

Colour flamed along her cheekbones. 'You know what sort of gossip that will cause.'

'Alas, gossip doesn't interest me.' He looked supremely indifferent to her accusing stare. 'Why should it upset you? It will soon be true.'

Quickly, fiercely, Melly bit out, 'You can't force me to sleep with you!'

'Darling heart, I could go in there with you and in ten minutes you'd be begging me to take you. Only that's not what I want.' His pale eyes glittered through the dark lashes as he leaned towards her still figure, saying softly, 'I want total surrender, Melissa, my ring on your finger, you bound to me by every tie I can manage. Then I'll discover just how much wildness there is behind that cool exterior. I want to see your eyes close in the agony that comes with passion, I want to see the pale gold satin of your skin heat with love's flush.'

Her blood thickened, caught fire. *'No,'* she whispered, appalled by the sudden triumphant blaze of tension his words and tone caused in her.

He laughed, mocking her, yet there was a deep sensual throb to his voice which revealed how he was enjoying her reaction. 'Don't hide your head in the sand,' he taunted. 'I'm going to lose myself in you, forget the grey years in the heat and passion of your body until I'm sated.'

Melly looked up, appalled again. 'You—you sound as though you hate me,' she faltered.

'Sometimes,' he said deliberately, holding her eyes with his, 'I think I do. But not enough to free you, sweetheart. You've held me chained for too long, I've grown to like my bonds. When you're as tightly roped as I am, when you've learned to love this prison we've made for each other—well, then I'll marry you.'

Worldlessly she turned away, unable to comprehend yet what he meant. From behind her he said, 'Melissa.'

She didn't answer, but she stopped, her tall slenderness held straight by willpower alone.

'Don't lie awake rationalising,' he advised silkily. 'And don't try to escape me. I'd follow you to hell.'

'Yet you couldn't get as far as London,' she said bitterly, betrayingly.

His hands on her shoulders made her gasp, but they pulled her back into the hard warmth of his body.

'The divorce has only just gone through,' his voice said as he nuzzled the lobe of her ear. 'You knew that, that's why you didn't come back before.'

She shivered at the erotic frisson his breath in her ear caused, but when she spoke her voice was cold and hard. 'What do you feed that ego on? Steak? I knew nothing——'

'Lie to yourself, but not to me.' He released her, pushing her away. 'Now get to bed. You sound exhausted.'

CHAPTER FOUR

EXHAUSTED Melly might have been, but it took her a long time to get to sleep. And in that time she did nothing constructive, merely lay in bed with heavy eyelids lowered over her hot eyes, while scraps of the night's conversation chased themselves around her brain. When she did sleep it was so soundly that the alarm ran down before she woke and she had to scramble out of bed with a thick head and not enough time to get ready.

As she showered and dressed she had no time to plan, none even to remember last night and the shocks she had received. Fortunately she had stocked the refrigerator with yoghurt. That obviated the need to make any breakfast, but she regretted the instant coffee which was all she had time for.

The sound of Trent's voice brought her head up with a jerk.

'What on earth,' he demanded, lounging in the doorway to the kitchen, 'is that revolting stuff you're eating?'

'Yoghurt.' She met his amused, sardonic expression with a glare. 'How did you get in? How dare you make yourself at home here?'

'There's actually very little I wouldn't dare,' he said thoughtfully, his eyes dancing. 'That's no sort of breakfast for a working woman!'

'I like it.' She put the little pot down defiantly.

'Ah well, I suppose I'd better stock up with some. Any particular sort?'

'Apricot and mango and pineapple——' Melly stopped her automatic recital of her favourites with a

64

snap, and an angry toss of her black curls. 'I asked you what you were doing here!'

'Making sure you're ready.'

'How did you get in?'

His brows lifted. 'You, my dearest love, were so tired you didn't bother to lock the door last night. Not a good idea. If you don't want me prowling in whenever I feel like it, you'd better remember.'

'Oh, I will, believe me,' she told him grimly.

He laughed at that, appreciating her sarcasm. 'Ready to go?'

'Just about.'

This time those who saw them arrive had distinctly speculative looks on their faces. Melly felt humiliated colour burn her cheeks and determined angrily to get herself a car as soon as possible.

That Trent was well aware of the interest they were rousing was quite obvious. In the empty lift he leaned a shoulder against the wall and grinned at her, the formal business suit emphasising his rangy body, the jacket open to reveal a waistcoat sexily hugging the tapering waist, lean legs in an indolent stance.

'You look as though flames could shoot out of the top of your head,' he taunted.

'You've put me in an impossible position.'

'Nonsense. You'll get quite accustomed to being taken for my girl-friend,' he said heartlessly.

Almost she ground her teeth. 'Mistress, you mean.'

'What a charming, old-fashioned turn of phrase you have!'

Fortunately her floor was next. Without a word she stepped out through the doors and walked away, but not before she heard his soft laughter behind her.

Fortunately she was kept too busy to think. When she ate lunch in the park down the street she was joined by Susan Field, her large eyes snapping with interest, and Melly mentally girded herself for an inquisition.

'How are things going?' Susan asked chattily, eyeing Melly's salad sandwich as though she was even curious about that.

'Well, I've enough work to keep me going for a month or so, and that's if no one used the library.'

Susan smiled. 'Oh, they'll use it,' she said knowingly. 'It's Mr Addison's pet project at the moment. The ukase has gone forth.' She spoke with mock dramatics, rolling her eyes, but she was dying with curiosity and it showed.

'I wish he'd given me time to get things straight,' Melly grumbled, finishing the rest of her sandwich in a gulp.

'Mr Addison? You're joking, of course. He doesn't believe in giving anyone time to do anything,' Susan informed her. 'I mean, when he says now, he means yesterday. And next week means within five minutes. Or so I've heard,' she finished lamely, her eager expression not in the least unkind.

Melly felt a certain sympathy for her. 'I believe you,' she sighed. 'My brother is a bit the same. Do you think it's the result of a boarding school education?'

She surprised an unrestrained chuckle out of the other girl. 'Somehow I doubt it. I think our Mr Addison is one on his own and it sounds rather as though your brother might be, too. What does he do?'

It was pleasant to sit in the sun and tell Susan a little of Te Puriri, while girls in their new summer dresses paraded past. This year the fashionable colours were warm, clear pastels, lemon and lime, apricots and pinks, a blue the exact colour of the sky. From a distance it looked as if the contents of one of the flower beds in the park had taken to the streets. Even those women who were choosing the comparatively calm time before the schools broke up to do their Christmas shopping looked cheerful and not at all harassed by the summer heat and the prospect of weeks of holidays as well as the hectic Christmas which most New Zealanders take for granted.

Reluctantly Melly said, 'Well, I suppose we'd better be getting back.'

And reluctantly Susan agreed. They walked beneath enormous trees as old as Auckland, planted by the very first settlers to ease some of the pangs of the homesickness that assailed them over a century ago in this strange Antipodean land, then out of the park and into the street, the heat striking back up from the concrete footpath.

As they passed a theatre Melly's head turned to read the advertising outside. One of Tom Stoppard's plays, one she'd missed.

'We're making up a party on Friday night,' Susan told her. 'Like to come?'

The tone, the words, were casual enough, but she couldn't hide her curiosity. She'd learned nothing this time; perhaps she hoped to find out more on Friday night. Lightly Melly said, 'Why not? I haven't seen that one. Who do I see about it?'

'Oh, I'll bring her round at afternoon tea.'

Melly hid a quick grimace. Rumour, she thought disgustedly, rumour and gossip. *Damn* Trent!

She bought her ticket and exchanged a pleasant few words with the girl Susan brought to see her, aware of more avid interest. As had happened yesterday, Trent's secretary contacted her to tell her sweetly that Trent had had to fly to Wellington for an emergency meeting, but that she would be driven home.

Which she was by a loquacious middle-aged man who told her that he was the caretaker and jack of all trades for the building. As he chatted on it became more than clear that he was Trent's man, viewing him with something like worship, if so irreverent an attitude could be called that. He was fiercely partisan, like a man watching a beloved grandchild grow up, but with the pride and respect went a refreshing lack of awe.

Interesting, she thought, as he told her that he was going back into town in a taxi. Ordered for him, of course, by Trent.

Well, probably by Trent's secretary, Melly decided, but if Mr Owen liked to think that it was Trent who had actually rung for the taxi, why disillusion him?

As she made a salad for her dinner, Melly found herself yawning. An early night and a good sleep would shift the faint depression she felt. And a phone call north.

An hour later she had heard her nephew's latest words, learned about the results of Jennet's last firing in the kiln Rafe had had constructed for his wife, and discussed with her brother the sort of car she needed. And she did feel better, but still slightly down, so she climbed into shorts and a T-shirt and her running shoes and set off for a run.

An hour later she came in, meeting again the woman who had given Trent such a blatant come-on in the lift the night before.

This time she was going out, elegant and sexy in black lace with the glimmer of diamonds in her ears and on her fingers. She gave a swift sideways smile at Melly, her mascaraed eyes flicking disparagingly over the long tanned legs and heated face.

The man with her was not so dismissive. It was appreciation that warmed his glance, the kind of assessment Melly knew very well. Wondering what she was like in bed, no doubt, she thought angrily. Men!

She should have been tired. Her day had been wearying; Trent's edict had seen a constant stream of visitors and calls to the library, most of whom had seemed quite surprised at the fact that she was able to help them. Combined with her efforts to get the place into better order, they had wearied her. Physically she was exhausted, yet when she was ready for bed she viewed it with disfavour. A book didn't help. Her eyes drooped over the page, but as soon as she put it down and switched off the lamp they stayed defiantly open. She stared out of the window while her brain told her she was a fool.

For she knew why she was possessed by this intolerable restlessness. Oh, she could repress the knowledge, she had been doing just that all evening, but alone in her big bed the busyness she had used as a barrier was gone and she faced the truth. Which was distasteful, hard to accept, but so obvious that she had to accept it.

She was waiting for Trent to come home.

She even said aloud, 'I am waiting for Trent to come back.'

Ridiculous. Yet according to popular psychology now that she had confronted her need, it should be alleviated. Or was it that she would be able to deal with it better?

Restlessly, her bones aching as though she had a fever, she twisted between the sheets until they felt hot and prickly. She could not cope with the idea that she needed Trent. Desired him, yes, that was easy enough. Why not? The raw intelligence and power that stamped the man made him incredibly attractive to women, as did the lean graceful body and that mocking provocative awareness. Oh yes, he didn't need classical features, he had more than enough offensive weapons in that department.

He was a very sexy man and she wanted him. But *needed* him? Desire was common coinage, you didn't have to like a man to want him. If you admitted to need, you were in danger because that meant he was entangled in the fabric of your life, a necessary part of it.

'No,' she said, quite calmly, and got up and poured some milk into a saucepan. While it heated she told herself reasonably that almost certainly Trent wouldn't be home tonight. He'd probably stay in Wellington overnight and catch the businessman's special up in the morning. That would be the sensible thing to do. So that was what Trent would do. After all, that cool, logical brain was fully in control of his life.

She only just managed to catch the milk before it rose clear of the saucepan. It took a few seconds of hasty blowing on the seething, unstable mass and an extremely rapid sideways jerk to control it. The irony of the situation made her smile. Trent's marriage had shown that he was able to bend his whole life to his will, using that crystalline intelligence to overwhelm the hunger of the heart and the body. And she couldn't even manage a pot of milk!

After a quick glance at her watch, she filled a beaker and walked back into the sitting-room. It was a bright night, no moon, but no cloud either, and the combination of city lights and stars made it unnecessary to switch on a lamp, so Melly stood at the window while she drank the milk, staring at the panorama beneath. Absently her eyes picked out the lines of lamps which denoted streets and roads, the dark patches of domains and parks, the house lights glowing softly behind curtains and blinds. The harbour was a sinuous blackness, an emptiness dotted with a few small constellations which signified small settlements on the islands.

At last, slightly chilly, Melly took her beaker out and washed it, then turned off the light in the kitchen and went to bed.

Somehow, when the phone went she wasn't surprised, although caution chilled her answer.

Sure enough, Trent's mocking tones asked, 'Miss me, Melissa?'

'That sounds,' she said pertly, 'like the title of a song. One that a barber's-shop quartet might sing.'

His deep chuckle pleasured her. 'Nice evasion, darling, but I want an answer.'

'I hardly had time to, did I.' Bother, that was *not* what she had intended to say. She added, 'Not that I would have, anyway.'

'Of course not.'

Hastily, before he could pursue the subject she asked, 'Where are you? I thought you'd stay overnight and come home in the morning.'

'No, darling, I like my own bed; especially when it's such a short distance from yours. At this moment we're about sixteen feet away from each other. Sixteen feet too far.'

Angrily Melly crashed the receiver back on to the telephone, hating the amusement in his voice, the slow, deliberate seduction in the words. If he rings again I won't answer, she thought, dragging the sheets over her shoulders as she huddled into the pillows, turning her back ostentatiously, quite ridiculously to the telephone.

But he didn't ring again.

The rest of the week passed quickly. Each day Melly went to work with Trent, each night he drove her home; he was his usual tormenting self, but he made no further attacks on her willpower, apparently content to keep a distance between them.

Melly didn't realise, not then and not for some time later, how skilfully he used that week to allay the fears his open and premature statement of his plans for her had aroused. It was as though the car became neutral ground; he was once more the Trent she had fallen in love with years ago, amusing, charming, his clever brain and quick wit making him the best companion in the world.

Without even thinking of it she learned to relax in his presence. Of course it was deliberate.

Trent was too calculating not to know exactly what he was doing, but Melly, ably encouraged by a traitor within of whose existence she was still unaware, managed to push into the recesses of her mind the fact that he would stop at nothing to get what he wanted.

She knew he wanted her, but she deluded herself into believing that because the memory of his previous betrayal was ever-present, she was safe from him.

On Friday evening he said abruptly, 'Get dressed and I'll take you out to dinner.'

It gave her some considerable pleasure to tell him with all the demureness at her disposal, 'Sorry, but I'm already going out tonight.'

She didn't miss the razor-sharp glance that cut across her profile or the harsh undertone in his voice as he asked, 'With whom?'

'With a party. We're going to the theatre.'

One lean finger tapped at the steering wheel as they sat at some lights. 'And afterwards?'

'Afterwards nothing.'

'I see. Who are you going with?'

Very quietly she said, 'Trent, that's none of your business. But I'm not going with anyone—there's a party of us.'

'Very well then, I'll rephrase it. Who is bringing you home?'

Sighing, she snapped, 'Nobody. I'll come home on the bus.'

'Like hell you will. It's too dangerous at that time of night. Cancel your booking and I'll take you.'

She began to protest, breaking off when she saw that he wasn't listening. Frowning, his eyes were fixed on the lights; he gave a grim nod as the red flashed into green.

Beginning again, Melly said icily, 'Trent, I'm going tonight. I want to go. And thousands of people travel on the buses every night with perfect safety, as you're well aware.'

'You have to walk over a hundred yards to get home from the nearest bus stop.'

Exasperation and resentment she kept hidden sharpened her features as she looked up at him. The fierce bone structure of his face was set into a ruthless determination that made her feel weak. She hated the sensation.

'Then I'll get a taxi,' she said angrily. 'There's a taxi stand fifty yards away from the theatre. I'll walk with everyone down to it and they can wait there until I've driven away. All right?'

'Of course,' he said calmly. 'Who are you going with?'

'A group from work. I doubt if you'd know any of them by name, they're from the lower echelons.'

The distinctly sarcastic note in her voice brought his head around. For a second his eyes raked her face before he switched his attention back to the road, saying mildly, 'As it happens, I can put a name to every face I see in the building.'

Melly felt half an inch high. 'How do you do it?' she groaned. 'No, don't tell me, I know I make it easy for you. They all think you're a wonderful boss.'

'Do they?'

She laughed at the dry disclaimer. 'By and large, yes. All the girls fancy you like mad, of course, and the men think anyone who's got where you are at such an early age is clearly a genius. And the word seems to be that although you have a tongue like a buzz-saw if anyone does anything stupid, you trust your employees and leave them to get on with their jobs. Provided they do their stuff properly, of course.'

'Of course.' The two words were delivered with an astringency that puzzled her until he continued, 'You, however, know that I got where I am today by nefarious deeds, don't you? Do you dispel their illusions with the details of my villainy?'

Melly bit her lip. 'No,' she said huskily. 'I owe you my loyalty as one of your employees.'

'In no other respect?'

Black curls swung heavily about her head as she shook it. She said nothing, conscious of a thickness in her throat.

'Ah well, we'll change that,' he said lightly, swinging the car into the drive of the apartment block.

'I doubt it.'

He smiled, the thin lips arrogantly confident. As he switched the engine off he leaned over and kissed her, quickly, brutally. Her lips quivered, then softened beneath the hard aggression of his mouth, just before he drew away from her. In the semi-darkness his narrowed eyes gleamed.

'Of course it will happen,' he said silkily. 'I'll have all of your loyalty, Melissa, every last little scrap of it. I told you I wanted everything you have to give, every waking thought, every night time dream, every breath you draw. So enjoy yourself tonight. Nights out without me are going to be a thing of the past very shortly.'

Shaken by the savage intensity in every blazing word, she fumbled at the door handle. Once she was safely outside she said defiantly, 'The days are long past when a man had the right to stamp around a woman's skull in his heavy boots. You know you can only get from me what I'm prepared to give you.'

Smoothly, efficiently, Trent locked up the car, his face expressing an amusement that made her jaw ache with her determination to keep her teeth clenched.

'That is, if I were prepared to hang around and wait for you to give,' he said as they started off towards the lift. 'Which I'm not, sweetheart. I prefer to take.'

'Just like a pirate!'

He chuckled. 'Just like a pirate. And like your average buccaneer I get short-tempered if I have to wait.'

'Are you threatening me, Trent?'

He met her steady black regard with a twisted smile. 'Yes, of course I am. Ah, here's the lift.'

And in it was a girl, small yet voluptuous, her flaming head of hair restrained into an elegant chignon, her vivid, beautiful face lighting up as she saw the man who waited for it.

'Trent!' Cathy Durrant said exuberantly. 'I was just on my way up to your apartment when you dragged the lift down here! How are you? You look as if it's been a tiring week. Poor darling, you sounded exhausted when you rang me.'

The husky sensual croon in the younger woman's voice made Melly feel sick to the depths of her soul. She felt the colour receding from her skin, met the swift upward glance from beneath Cathy's lashes and knew how she must look.

Then Trent's hand clasped her elbow, urged her into the lift, and slowly the blood began beating through her body again.

'Melissa, have you met Cathy?' said Trent, his voice level.

Melly shook her head, but Cathy said sharply, 'You're Melly Hollingworth, aren't you? I know your brother Rafe. And his wife. I was at their wedding with my grandmother and grandfather, but I don't suppose you remember me.'

'I'm afraid I don't.' Melly was rather encouraged by the cool restraint of her tone, so encouraged that she tried for a smile and almost got there. 'I was so busy being a bridesmaid that the rest of the wedding rather passed me by.'

Cathy smiled sunnily at her, apparently not in the least surprised to see her ex-husband escorting Melly. 'I know what it's like, I was chief bridesmaid for my cousin and I spent the entire wedding being terrified that something awful would happen. It did, too. The pageboy got tiddly on champagne and had to be taken off kicking and swearing diabolically to sleep it off! But at least it didn't happen to me!'

And that was all that mattered, her tone implied. Through her pain Melly recognised that for Cathy, that was all that had mattered. Self-centred, she thought dimly as Trent made an observation that brought a peal of laughter from Cathy; self-centred as hell, but oh, so beautiful.

She could not look at Trent, she was too afraid to see what light gleamed in the hard clarity of his eyes when he looked at Cathy. That they were on the best of terms was obvious; what then had caused the divorce?

And why had Trent rung her up and asked her to come to his apartment?

Questions like horrible black blowflies buzzed shrilly about in Melly's head, but she had to smile and nod and pretend to be perfectly normal, and at last get out of the lift and leave them together, Cathy's long varnished nails resting lightly, confidingly on the dark stuff of Trent's sleeve, her voice beginning before the lift doors had closed, that damned, intimate, laughing note in it.

Melly had never believed that she had anything in her of the Hollingworth temper, that black fury which made her half-brother so forbidding when it was aroused, but now she was overcome with it, a terrible primitive need to strike out at its source. For long seconds she stood trembling, her hands clenched at her sides, fighting it. Visions of Cathy's lovely, seductive face swirled in a red mist, the laughter wiped from it by some action of Melly's, tears forming in the great blue eyes.

'Oh God,' she whispered, horrified by her capacity for anger and the dark images of revenge on a woman who had done nothing to her.

She would not submit, she would not surrender to this savage insane fury!

But it took her long minutes to force it back into her subconscious. Slowly, walking heavily, she went into the kitchen and drew a jug of orange juice from the refrigerator, forcing herself to think about what she was doing while she poured a glass. As the icy liquid slid pleasantly over her tongue and down a throat parched and rough, she deliberately wooed the sanely logical part of her brain, coaxing reason into being instead of the fierce irrational passion which had flushed her brain.

It worked. Ruthlessly refusing to speculate on what was happening in the penthouse apartment, she went into her bedroom and got into her running clothes, intent on dispelling the remnants of that frightening anger with activity.

That worked, too. An hour and a half later she was standing exhausted under the shower, thinking dismally that going out was the last thing she wanted to do! Still, after the shower and a sketchy but appetising dinner, she felt better, less like a limp rag, and by the time she had dressed and made up her face the effects of that firestorm of emotion had almost been hidden.

The play was excellent, witty and satirical and sharp, well acted by the local company. After it was over they all went to a coffee bar and drank coffee and flirted and exchanged opinions and made plans for further outings. Melly mentioned her decision to take a taxi, and Susan promptly organised her a ride home with an extremely pleasant man who had been watching Melly with interest for the entire evening.

'Ian Sanderson,' Susan said cheerfully. 'Melly Hollingworth. Ian, you go out Melly's way, don't you?'

'Yes, of course.' Only three words, but the intonation made it plain that even if he hadn't been, he would have gladly gone out of his route to take Melly home.

Melly accepted gracefully, smiling her thanks. Perhaps this would put an end to those rumours that saw her as Trent's mistress.

All in all, a pleasant evening. Ian was good company and drove well. For a moment Melly found herself toying with the idea of getting him to put her out a little farther down the road, but she rejected the idea almost as soon as it occurred. She wasn't ashamed of living in The Towers and it was unlikely that many people knew that Trent lived there too.

When she gave her address Ian's brows lifted, but before he could comment she explained, 'I'm living in my brother's flat. It seemed a pity to let it waste.'

'I'll say!' he agreed fervently. 'Do we have to produce proof of identity at the gate?'

She chuckled. 'No, security is pretty tight, but not that severe. The doorman checks us in and out, I think, until a certain time, and after that we have keys.'

'Sounds impressive. Not like New Zealand, though.'

'Well, no, but that's the way things are going, I'm afraid.'

Their discussion on the causes for the rising crime rate took them into the grounds of the building. When the engine was switched off in the visitors' parking lot Melly said, 'Would you like a cup of coffee? Or did you have enough at the coffee bar?'

Ian's face signalled that her message had been received and understood. If he came in, it would be for coffee only.

He laughed. 'I can always go a second cup of coffee. And I must confess I'd like to see what's inside this building. Also, of course, get to know you a little better without a horde of fellow-workers watching every movement.'

Melly said lightly, 'Then come on up,' her mind switching back to Susan's hissed information before they left.

'He's a sweetie,' she had told Melly, 'I've been out with him, and he keeps his hands to himself and doesn't get drunk and can conduct an intelligent conversation. Everyone likes him.'

And he certainly seemed an honest, trustworthy soul. Not madly exciting, but then, Melly decided as they

walked across the lobby under the doorman's watchful
eye, you couldn't have everything.

He admired the apartment, and the view, talking
easily about it while she put the percolator on. And
then the telephone rang.

'Sorry,' said Melly, frowning as she picked up the
receiver. 'Hello?'

'What the devil have you been doing?'

Trent's voice, icily restrained.

Melly's eyes widened, then narrowed. Tactfully Ian
had taken himself off to the other side of the sitting-
room.

'Do you realise it's after midnight——' she began,
only to be interrupted.

'Yes, I do. I also realise that the theatre closed at ten
forty-five. I rang and asked them. Where have you been
since then?'

'Drinking coffee in a coffee bar. Good night.'

It took a considerable amount of willpower not to
slam the receiver back on to the handset, but she
achieved it. She also achieved a wry smile for a patently
interested Ian.

'Some people,' she told him sweetly, 'don't seem to
realise the time!'

But the damage had been done. She could see all the
rumours adding up in his head, and could only admire
the adroitness with which he took his leave, coffee-less
and probably feeling he'd had a very narrow escape.

Five minutes later Melly was busy scrubbing her
teeth in the bathroom, thinking longingly of several
extremely unpleasant things she would like to do to
Trent Addison, involving thumbscrews and boiling oil
and water tortures.

CHAPTER FIVE

AND although she slept well, when Melly awoke the next morning the same thoughts were predominant in her mind, so much so that after she had re-heated last night's spurned coffee and drunk it, brooding over Trent's perfidy, she stormed out of the apartment and into the lift with only one thing on her mind. She was, she decided grimly, going to let him know that his interference in her life was not only not wanted but bitterly resented.

It wasn't until she had pressed the doorbell with several sharp jabs that she remembered Cathy Durrant. Who quite possibly was still there. Too late, she thought idiotically, her anger draining from her in a flood of pain. It was too late to flee back down to her own apartment.

Trent opened the door with suspicious swiftness as though he'd been waiting for her. He grinned into her face and said, 'Ah, I expected you this morning, but not quite so early. Come for a swim?'

Melly's anger returned, augmented by fury at the mocking appreciation in the grey eyes as they swept her face.

'No, thank you,' she snapped, standing still. She wasn't going in there until she was convinced that he was alone.

'It might cool you down.' He lifted a brow at the mutinous expression on her face and said, 'O.K., you want to get it off your chest. Come in and shout at me.'

Almost she ground her teeth, a childish habit she had overcome years ago. Her anger, however, gave her the courage to demand, 'Is there anyone in there?'

He looked a little startled at that, but he was too shrewd not to understand. 'Cathy went home an hour after she arrived,' he said blandly, 'and contrary to gossip, I do not consider a night wasted if I don't bed someone. I have the normal appetites, but I like to think I have a certain amount of self-control and quite frankly, I find promiscuity distasteful.'

'But not marrying for ulterior reasons,' she flung back at him, wanting only to tip him off that infuriating plateau of self-control he seemed to inhabit.

She succeeded. His eyes darkened and he jerked her through the open door by the wrists, saying between his teeth, 'Obviously not, you little prig. Now, say what you want to say. Just remember, I do have a temper to match that black Hollingworth one of yours, and if you goad me too far I'll make you feel it.'

'How?' she jibed, hiding the first tremor of fear. 'Beat me?'

'Don't tempt me.' He hadn't released her wrist, now he turned into the sitting-room, pulling her with him across the pale floor towards the end of the kitchen which had been set up as a second sitting-room and casual dining area. Sunlight poured cheerfully in through the windows and the wide glass doors opened out on to the roof garden, and over it all, the kitchen and the pleasant, comfortable room, was the delicious smell of bacon and perking coffee.

Melly said angrily, 'You had no right to ring me last night and you know it! How the hell did you know when I got home?'

'Because I'd been ringing every ten minutes for an hour,' he told her, pushing her into a chair.

The table had been set for breakfast. As Melly saw the toast and kiwi-fruit jam and honey, her stomach made it embarrassingly clear that she had not yet eaten. But not even hunger was going to take her mind off her grudge.

'Why?' she demanded, infuriated all over again. 'My God, you've got a nerve! You——'

'Who was he?' Trent asked quietly, walking across to attend to the bacon.

Melly's chin lifted. 'None of your business!'

He slid the slices from the oven on to a plate already decorated with eggs and grilled tomatoes and brought it back to the table.

'I could,' he said, as he put a slice of bacon, an egg and half a tomato on to another plate, 'tell you at great length that I've made you my business. I won't, because I think enough of your intelligence to know that you're well aware of that fact. However, I'll give you one piece of advice. This battle is a private one. Don't drag anyone else into it unless you want to see him messily removed from the field. Now, who did you have with you last night?' He slid the plate across to her.

'Do you expect me to tell you after that rather histrionic threat?' she asked scornfully.

He got up again and brought back from a sideboard the necessary silver. 'Salt?'

'No, thank you.'

She was too hungry not to eat, but she was not going to let him put her off. Sneaking a look from beneath her lashes, her eyes were caught and held by the curiously cold impact of his.

'I'll find out,' he said calmly.

'I shouldn't have thought that snooping was your style,' Melly returned with all the contempt she could muster.

He suddenly seemed much older, much more remote than she had ever seen him. 'I'll do anything I have to,' he said indifferently. 'Why look so surprised, Melissa? That's what you believe, isn't it? That I'm a cold, calculating bastard, intent on acquiring power by whatever means I can, however devious and dishonest they are?'

'If I think that I have good reason.' Her voice was shaking but she firmed it and went on, 'Can't you just leave it, Trent? I know what you want of me, but I don't think there's anything you could do which would make me trust you again. I'm sorry, but when—if I marry, it will be someone who considers me the most important thing in his life.'

Her anger had gone, leaving her as tired as he looked. Quietly she finished, 'Not a man who wouldn't think twice about throwing me out if the chance to acquire even more power was contingent on him being wifeless.'

She watched the way his fingers clenched on to the fork he was holding until the knuckles pressed whitely against the dark skin. So she could make him suffer, she thought, and wondered why she wasn't exhilarated by the knowledge. Perhaps it was because she hated to see that sharply honed bleakness in his face; she wanted to comfort him, to take back the words which had fallen from her unruly tongue and tell him that she didn't mean them. Of its own volition her hand lifted towards him, then fell.

She could not give him the surrender he wanted so badly.

Trent had been staring down at the table, but the swift incautious movement of her hand brought his head up. Melly shrank back as she read the blazing purpose in his face, that thrilled her while it raised the hairs on her skin in the old, atavistic prelude to panic.

'Then you'll just have to change your mind,' he said evenly, 'because I'm now changing mine. If I have to, I'll hunt you down, Melissa, until you're too tired to keep on running.'

'You're mad,' she whispered, terrified.

He grinned at that, that slashing pirate's grin, but above it his eyes were cold and flat and un-compromising.

'No,' he said. 'I just know what I want. I've always known what I've wanted.'

'I suppose I should be flattered.'

The broad shoulders lifted in a small shrug. 'Why? Because I want you? What flattery is there in that? I don't want to, believe me.'

She didn't like that, but she understood how he felt. She knew all about the kind of nagging need that ached and ached, smearing the world so that everything was dull and joyless, without savour or grace. That was how things had been for her until she had walked across the lobby and seen Trent again. Then the world had blazed out in all its bright colours and she had tasted delight on her tongue.

Panic-stricken, her mind refused to accept the evidence of her senses. For if Trent did this to her she must love him; all the years between, the steady ascendancy of logic over emotions were wiped away by a love she did not want. With the incandescent response, the vivid awareness that ran through her body like a quicker, more vital bloodstream, there was pain and bitter resentment and fear.

'Then put me out of your mind,' she said in a hard little voice.

'I've tried, and it doesn't work.' He smiled without humour, his severe bone-structure suddenly prominent beneath the fine tanned skin. 'You are in my blood, a necessary part of me. I can no more rid myself of you than I could tear me heart out of my body. God knows why, I've met more beautiful women, more sophisticated, certainly more seductive, but from the first time I saw you it's been only you. I have to have you. And I'm going to.'

The colour receded from her skin, leaving her cold and shaken. Beneath the steely self-control there had been such stark hunger that she had to believe him. Her lips fell apart, but the words of denial which she wanted to say would not be articulated.

He stared at the play of muscles in her long throat,

then lifted his glance to meet hers. And Melly was afraid all over again, for the crystalline clarity of his eyes was gone, replaced by a flaring need that darkened them into menace.

'If you'd married while you were overseas I'd have come and taken you,' he said quietly. 'If you get involved with anyone else I'll break it up. I don't care how much humiliation I make you suffer. I don't care what your friends or your family say or do. You belong to me, and when you admit that, we'll be married. Until then you're on a very short string, so don't forget it. And no more invitations like last night's.'

Melly's face was white, her narrowed eyes dark slivers of glittering obsidian. 'You can threaten me all you like,' she flung at him through colourless lips, 'but I am not your slave or plaything and I'll do exactly what I want to, when I want to and with whom I want.' Her voice broke. She steadied it, meeting his heavy-lidded gaze with such blind fury that she could have hit him, beaten him to the floor. 'I don't think I've ever despised anyone as much as I do you. Do you really think you can use this stupid physical attraction to force me into marriage? I'd rather die!'

The chair scraped across the tiles as she pushed it back and stood up. Quick as she was, he was there before she could take more than a couple of steps away from the table.

She expected him to meet her fury with his own, so she stiffened when his hands fell on to her shoulders, her rage beating up to confront his.

He was smiling, the thin lips curved in amusement, dangerous, reckless as the buccaneer he always was in her fantasies.

'Darling,' he said smoothly, fierce laughter crackling like lightning in his eyes, in his voice, 'you want me as vehemently as you hate me. One day all that fire and fury will be mine.'

He believed it. He really believed it, and she could
have hit him, because beneath her anger and contempt
there was a chilling realisation that she had pitifully few
defences against such ruthless determination. He had
only to hold her like this, fingers biting into her
shoulders, and her body flamed into awareness, the
memory of him imprinted so deeply that she recalled
exactly how it felt to be crushed in his arms.

Sooner or later she would be overcome by need and
she would agree to marry him. Then he would have
what he wanted. He would take her, invade all the
secret places of her body and her mind, reduce her to a
dependency the thought of which scared her witless.

It was not pride that kept her from surrendering, not
anger because he had jilted her. It was a matter of
survival, a primitive instinct that warned her that he
had the power to reduce her to a cypher.

Except for her father, a gentle man dominated by her
mother, Melly had grown up in a family of
exceptionally strong characters. Rafe was as tough as
whipcord and Jennet was strong too, strong enough to
face everyone's disapproval when she had come back to
prevent Melly from marrying Derek. Melly had always
hoped that she had the Hollingworth strength while
avoiding the family temper. Now she realised that she
was as weak as water. She had to be, to be
contemplating marriage with Trent.

'You're a bully,' she said in a voice that trembled.

'Because you force me to be.' He was implacable.

When she shook her head he kissed her and the slow,
sensuous movement of his mouth over hers made her
gasp with desire and pain. He could have used the
involuntary opening of her mouth to deepen the kiss.
She expected him to; she wanted him to, but he lifted
his head and as well as the passion she expected there
was a tenderness and sympathy in his expression.

'My poor girl,' he said, pulling her against him so

that her head rested on his shoulder. 'Don't make me wait too long, my lovely. I'm not normally a patient man.'

'That sounds like another threat.'

She felt the sigh he gave. 'I'm rather afraid it might be. See what you've made me sink to! Threatening a woman!'

She responded to the self-derisory note in his voice with a confession she shouldn't have made. 'Well, you are the only man who summons the Hollingworth temper in me.'

Her voice tailed away as he pushed her from him, narrowed gaze gleaming with a satisfaction he didn't try to hide.

'Good. Now sit down and finish your breakfast and I'll take you out for the day.'

Wearily, feeling as though she was carrying a load too big for her shoulders, Melly shook her head. 'No, Trent.'

'I'm sailing.'

He knew how she enjoyed it, but she met his eyes squarely. 'No.'

That sharp, confident grin lifted the hairs on the back of her neck. Quite softly he said, 'Then you'd better go, pretty girl, before I forget myself and spend the rest of the day showing you my bedroom.'

Almost she responded to his challenge. It hurt to dampen down the quick surge of ire his arrogant self-confidence sparked in her, but she was afraid. He knew her weaknesses better than she did herself and if he set out to seduce her there would be a toss-up as to who won.

So she said evenly, 'Sorry, but I have things to do.'

'Such as?'

'Buying a car,' she told him, something of her triumph showing in her tone.

That hateful amusement showed once more as he nodded. 'What sort?'

'Well, Rafe said——' She told him what Rafe had said, and somehow she found herself sitting opposite him again, not only finishing the breakfast he had cooked for her, but also drinking excellent coffee while they discussed suitable cars and the places to buy them.

Like this he was too easy to like, Melly thought at one stage, but she couldn't summon the necessary willpower to leave. And when he said briskly, 'Right, run down and do whatever's necessary, I'll pick you up in half an hour,' it took her quite a few seconds before she realised just how completely he had taken the initiative.

'What about your sailing?' she protested.

The broad shoulders lifted in a shrug. 'Not to worry. I wasn't intending to race.'

'But your crew . . .'

'I sail single-handed.' He smiled. 'I'm not a team man, Melissa. I prefer to take responsibility for my own actions.'

'It must make being a tycoon difficult,' she said.

'On occasions I have to do violence to my own inclinations,' he agreed, apparently not at all put out by her waspish comment. 'However, the ultimate responsibility is still mine, so all the gains and all the losses are also mine.'

'Are there many losses?' she asked.

'I lost you. Temporaily.' His light observation was belied by the hard glance that accompanied it.

He was daring her to object and she responded coolly. 'Time will tell there, won't it? And I don't want you to come with me, Trent.'

'I know,' he said sympathetically. 'You'll have to overcome this aversion to my company that you've developed over the years. It's not normal in a married couple. People will begin to wonder.'

Melly bit her lip, torn by the need to laugh and shriek at the same time, well aware that he was watching her with a wry understanding that infuriated her.

'Never mind,' he said, turning her towards the door. 'It will work out, believe me.'

Meant to be reassuring, no doubt. Perhaps he had seen a glimpse of the bewildered confusion beneath the coolness she tried so hard to assume.

Melly was tall, with the long Hollingworth bones and the wide Hollingworth shoulders. Over the years she had realised that this limited her appeal; most men, she had decided cynically, liked to feel protective of the women they took out. It was difficult for them to feel at all protective of a woman who was built rather like an Amazon. Yet when Trent stood beside her she felt safe, as though nothing could ever hurt her. It wasn't the fact that he was six inches taller than she was, either. It wasn't the broad shoulders or the power that animated his lean, rangy body. Now, as she walked beside him to the door she realised that it was the unmistakable air of competence he wore like an aura. Reduced to its most basic level, Trent looked as though there was nothing he could not deal with. He inspired confidence.

A very useful quality in a business tycoon, she thought caustically.

Aloud she asked, 'If a UFO landed in front of you, what would you do?'

He chuckled, but gave the matter serious thought before replying, 'Be very careful, I'm afraid. Remove myself and anyone else around as far as possible away and wait for whatever was inside to make contact.'

She nodded, and he said with a glimmer of laughter, 'Have I passed a test, Melissa?'

'No,' she said lightly, but in a way he had. 'I wish . . .' she began, but her voice faded as she realised what she had been intending to say.

I wish the last years had never happened. I wish I could trust you. I wish you loved me.

'Wishing is a fool's pastime unless you're prepared to work to make your wishes come true, and often, even then.' Trent's voice was steely, as was the glance he gave her. 'Don't fall into that trap, darling. It's too seductive, and life's too short to be chasing will-o'-the-wisps. Settle for reality. Less fun, perhaps, but infinitely more satisfying. And with far less chance of bringing things crashing around your head.'

Her curiosity was stirred by the bleak note in his voice, but when she glanced upwards his face was serene. Yet he sounded—disillusioned, she thought fancifully, and found herself shivering. Cathy? Perhaps, or perhaps he had discovered for himself that short-cuts to power were a grim let-down.

Then he smiled, that quick, devil-may-care smile which was perhaps a mask he assumed to prevent anyone approaching too close to the man who lived behind the mask.

'Half an hour,' he said. 'Want me to see you to your door?'

'Don't be an idiot!'

He summoned the lift, saying just before it arrived, 'Don't stand me up, Melissa.'

'What would you do if I did?'

His mouth tightened. 'Drag you out.'

'And how could you do that?' she asked on a jeer.

'Quite easily.' He traced the outline of her mouth with a finger that intruded between her lips to touch the soft vulnerable skin inside her cheek. Melly stiffened at the intimate little caress, but couldn't draw away, her eyes wide and held by his.

'I own The Towers,' he told her softly. 'I can get into any one of the apartments if I need to.'

'*Own* it? But why? When?'

'I bought it as soon as your brother leased his apartment.' His gaze mocked her astonishment. 'I told you that if necessary I'd hunt you down, darling, but I've been doing it for some years. Buying this place was a step on the way.'

Before she could formulate any sort of reply the lift arrived and he put her into it. As the doors closed she saw that he was smiling with a hard irony which made her go cold all over because she felt so helpless.

It took her all the half-hour he had allowed her to persuade herself out of running. And it was only because she knew there was nowhere she could go. Her first instinctive thought had been to turn to Rafe for help, but it was not fair to embroil him in this. If she did it would be all-out war between him and Trent, and she shuddered at the thought. Both were tough, hard men; the result of such a situation would be no foregone conclusion, but Jennet would worry. After all, Melly thought robustly, she was now twenty-four, old enough to take care of herself.

She hoped. It was not as though Trent could force her into marriage. He had said he didn't want an affair and she believed him, so she really didn't have anything to worry about.

'Let's be modern,' she said to her reflection as she checked it, 'even if you do have an affair with him, what is there to worry about? Everyone has affairs now; you're just a late developer.'

But her bones seemed to liquefy at the thought and her face was sombre as she turned away. In his arms she was someone else, a woman so wanton that coherent thought was impossible; she thought with her senses, reacting only to the special male scent, the warmth and hardness of his body, the seductive expertise of his mouth and the delicate, sensuous touch of his hands on her.

Just thinking of it made her body flame with a need that ate into her self-possession. Slowly, her head flung back and eyes soft and slumbrous beneath half-closed lids, she ran her hand from her breasts to her waist while sensations rioted throughout her. Her hands dropped away, she stared at the woman in the mirror while self-contempt replaced the sensual appreciation which had flared like a beacon from her.

'Oh, *God*,' she muttered as she turned away to pick up her bag.

The hours that followed were almost an anti-climax. Gone was the threat of determined pursuit; Trent treated her as though she was an old friend. Well, perhaps not quite. She was willing to bet that he didn't exhibit such a strongly possessive streak towards any of his friends. Some unregenerate part of her ignored any feminist promptings and enjoyed it. When he asked what sort of car she wanted she said, 'Something small, but not too small. I have to be able to fit my long legs into it. And not a new one, because I can't afford one.' She met his raised brows with a shrug. 'My outgoings last quarter were fairly heavy.'

'Presents?'

Melly nodded wryly, thinking of the treasures which were still on the high seas. Exquisite things for Jennet, a picture by a modern artist for Rafe which had cost an enormous amount, a selection of toys for Dougal. As well as the things she couldn't resist for herself. The end results of a shopping spree she hadn't been able to resist.

'Want a loan?'

Melly reacted with a vigorous shake of her head and a frosty negative.

Trent laughed, 'Afraid of what I'll demand as security?' he said, and laughed again at the swift, fiery glance that stabbed down his profile. 'No, don't explode, I was teasing. Who taught you not to go into hock?'

'Diana,' she said on a sigh. Her mother had been incapable of managing on the very generous income she had received from the trust, so much so that on occasions she had been reduced to asking for help from Rafe. It was when he refused to act any more as her banker that she had married again, choosing a besotted and extremely wealthy man who had made irrelevant the fact that by doing so she had forfeited her income from the trust. Rafe and Diana had never liked each other, and Rafe's anger had intimidated even his lovely spoiled stepmother.

'Yes, I can imagine,' Trent said drily. 'A very expensive lady, your mother.'

There was nothing to say to that. Disloyal though she felt, Melly had to nod.

'Why do you work?' Trent probed. 'I'm sure you don't need to.'

'I'd be bored out of my mind in six months. I like working.'

The dark head nodded slowly. 'I understand that.' And he began to talk of the early days of his business career when he had been parlaying a small legacy from his mother into a thriving electronics business. Fascinated, Melly listened to a saga which was entertaining, at times hilarious, occasionally fraught with all the excitement of a thriller.

The enchantment lasted. He took her to an enormous used-car complex and entered into her search with complete enthusiasm, peering beneath bonnets and into boots, treating the occasion with a combination of professionalism and the enthusiasm of any normal male confronted by more cars then he can count and the possiblity of buying one.

Once she muttered, 'Do you know *anything* about cars?' and had to smother a chuckle when he returned just as softly, 'About as much as the average man.'

'Then I'd better get the A.A. to check before I buy anything.'

'Stupid not to.'

At this juncture their attendant salesman excused himself to take a telephone call, saying, 'Glen here will look after you while I'm gone.' He hesitated before explaining rapidly and a little bashfully, 'I took my wife to the maternity home last night and this is probably them now.'

'Oh, you must go,' Melly said, smiling, watching him as he made his swift way up to the office.

Glen was a totally different prospect. Only too eagerly he had embraced the philosophy of the hard sell; Melly noticed the quick, comprehensive glance with which he summed them up, the faint hint of insolence as he noted Trent's expensively casual clothes, the way his glance lingered on her breasts and the line of her thigh beneath the light cotton dress.

Apparently satisfied, he began to give them a spiel, rattling on about the merits of the car they were inspecting. After a short time Trent said, quite pleasantly, 'We'll look at this by ourselves, thank you.'

'Oh, but . . .'

Trent lifted his head and looked at the man. 'Thank you,' he said.

That was all, but Glen stopped as if he'd been hit by lightning. Fascinated, Melly watched as beads of sweat sprang out across his brow. She didn't dare look at Trent, although she was intensely curious to know exactly what it was about him which had so intimidated the salesman. She even felt a little sorry for him. However, he made quite a good recovery, smiling although with considerably less panache, before moving away to what he apparently considered a safe distance.

Only then did Melly's dark gaze move to Trent's face. It revealed nothing, not anger nor distaste nor irritation, yet she felt a cold shiver pull over her skin as she hurried into speech.

'What on earth did you do to him?' she asked, stupidly.

'Looked at him.' His voice was flat, without intonation or expression.

'Don't ever look at me like that, will you? Do you strip paint off at fifty paces for an encore?'

He grinned and tucked her hand into his arm, comforting her with the hard warmth of his body. 'If forced to it, and no, I won't ever look at you like that. He was being a nuisance, and I didn't like the way he leered at you.'

'You noticed,' she said with resignation.

'I notice everything about you.'

Fortunately the original salesman arrived back then, over the moon because his wife had presented him with a daughter.

'We've already got two boys,' he told them, 'so the little one was just what the doctor ordered!'

And Trent couldn't have been nicer, not then, not later when they finally decided on a car, subject to various tests and checks. As they were being escorted out he handed an envelope across to the salesman with the injunction to spend the contents on his wife.

He cut short the man's astonished thanks and tucked Melly's hand inside his elbow again, walking out with the natural arrogant grace which attracted more than a few feminine eyes about the enormous lot.

'That was nice,' Melly told him softly.

'I am nice!'

He meant her to laugh and she did, but some part of her wondered wistfully if it was true, if his hunger for power could co-exist with the thoughtfulness he had just revealed, as well as the pure male aggression which had frightened Glen off.

He was a disturbing, complex man and she knew he had few scruples; could she ever learn to accept the dark side of his character?

Biting her lip, she kept her eyes lowered, walking through groups of people without seeing them, her mind's eye filled with visions of the man who walked beside her while she struggled to banish from her consciousness the question she had just asked herself. If once she started to weaken, she was lost, and she could not afford that. Last time had shattered her, spoiling her trust in all men so that she refused to open herself to the possibility of another such betrayal. If she followed the urges of her heart and body and surrendered she would live in fear in case he did it again. His marriage had proved once and for all how little love meant to him. His loyalty had been sold for the opportunity to seize power, and if it happened after he had seduced her into his life again, she would be desperately bereft.

It was ironic, really. Had she been less demanding, if she was able to accept this ravishing physical attraction and their easy, affectionate companionship without seeking any more, a marriage between them would probably have every chance of success.

But she was greedy. She wanted more than sexual fireworks and companionship: she wanted the kind of love she had seen in Rafe's eyes when he looked at Jennet. Because she was able to give that intensity of love herself she would be bitterly unhappy if she did not receive it.

And she had only to lift her eyes to Trent's profile as she did now, to see the stark uncompromising self-sufficiency there and realise that if she was stupid enough to surrender to his pursuit she would know sensual gratification and affection and that was all. Trent was not a man to admit any woman to the central core of his being. He had spoken of his desire for her, his hunger, but since her arrival back in New Zealand he had not said anything about love.

And while she respected his honesty it hurt as if her heart had been bound in barbed wire to think that he understood so little of her character that he believed she would be satisfied with so little of him.

She was still looking up at him when a voice loudly pronounced her name, jerking her head sideways.

'Oh—Sara!' It took a moment for her to collect her wits. 'What are you doing roaming the streets?'

Her old school friend grinned, her eyes flicking obviously from Melly to Trent and back again. 'Window shopping,' she said. 'Jim has this dream that one day he'll have made enough money to buy a Rolls, so every so often we come down her to check them over and decide which one to get.'

'A *Rolls*?'

Sara's laughter joined Melly's. 'Well, not a new one, of course, and occasionally he changes his mind and veers towards a Ferrari or a Porsche, but he thinks a Rolls has the right establishment image.'

Who is this man? her eyes demanded. With resignation Melly introduced them, and then Jim, Sara's husband, when he emerged from his reverent admiration of something very long and sleek and expensive.

They recognised Trent's name; Jim's brows lifted slightly before he shook hands and Sara gave Melly an intimate woman's signal of appreciation. For a while they chatted pleasantly in the sun until Sara invited them back for coffee, flirting lightly with Trent, who smiled into her piquant face with open appreciation and accepted for them both.

CHAPTER SIX

'PLEASANT couple,' said Trent back in the Daimler.

Melly nodded, prey to a complex of emotions. She was pleased because Sara and Jim were so clearly impressed and yet that fact irritated her too. She was, she decided ruefully, scratchy.

'Sara and I went to school together. Jim is a lawyer. He's a partner with his father, but he spends quite a lot of his time at a neighbourhood law office. They're both darlings.'

'Jim Horning. I think I know his father. R. F. Horning?'

'Yes, that's him. He's a Q.C. and very, very fierce.'

'Ah yes, I've met him.'

At her enquiring glance Trent elaborated, 'He has represented the firm. A sound man.'

Quite obviously he wasn't going to tell her any more. And there was no reason to feel piqued, she told herself sternly. But she was.

Sara and Jim lived in splendid disorder in a huge old kauri villa which had at some stage of its life been converted into three flats and was now being reconverted into a house. Progress was slow as they liked doing as much as possible themselves, but they had finished the back of the house and a large entertainment area outside, so the more formal part could afford to wait.

'Until we get the money,' Sara confided as she put coffee in the percolator.

'And the time.' Jim was gloomy, but when Trent evinced interest in what they had done he cheered up and took him out to show him the pool complex.

As soon as they were out of the door Sara hissed in a conspirator's whisper, 'He's absolutely gorgeous, Mel, but are you sure you know what you're doing? I mean . . .'

'I know what you mean.' Sara knew a little of what had transpired three years ago. Melly ran a hand through her hair, frowning, wondering how to explain.

Before she could continue Sara said anxiously, 'I don't want to butt in. You know what you're doing, I'm sure.'

Did she? Aloud Melly said drily, 'I wish I could be sure of that.'

'I suppose . . . Do you think he's been in love with you all this time? That his marriage was just a temporary aberration? I mean, Cathy is terribly, terribly sexy, even if she was spoiled rotten . . .' Melly's wry smile made Sara's voice trail away, but she made a swift recovery. 'I don't,' she finished firmly, 'believe the tales that went around about him marrying her to get control of the Durrant group. Even Jim's father said the holdings were more of a liability than a blessing!'

'But not now.'

'Well, no. But he must have worked himself into the ground to get the business back on its feet. It was all pretty unpleasant. I remember reading in the paper about it, the shake-up and the sackings and all the manoeuvring to and fro until Mr Addison made his position secure.'

Melly moved across the room to stand before two french windows leading on to the terrace. With eyes narrowed against the bright sunlight outside, she watched the two men as they walked around the pool towards a small building which housed the pump and filtration unit as well as garden tools. Trent's lean-hipped stride covered the ground with an easy unforced grace that made Jim, a little less in height, seem blocky and almost awkward.

Sara came to stand behind her, peering over her shoulder.

'Perhaps,' said Melly in a voice that didn't sound like hers, 'I'm rest and recreation for the warrior after the battle.'

'Do you still love him? Don't answer that if you don't want to.'

Melly watched the sun strike sparks of red from Trent's bent head. 'I don't know,' she admitted on an expelled breath. 'All I know is that I'm not going to get hurt again. I've had as much pain as I care to take from him.'

'He doesn't strike me as being a cruel man.' Sara spoke reflectively, her vivid little face thoughtful and wise. 'Hard, tough as leather, but not deliberately cruel. At least not in his private life.'

'You know him so well?'

'Well, word gets around. Oh, we don't move in the same circles, he's way out of our sphere, but Jim's father knows that crowd, the really rich, old money. Not that Papa Horning's indiscreet, he's not, but you can usually tell what he thinks of people. And, as I said, word gets around.'

'And what does Mr Horning think of Trent?'

'He respects him,' Sara said simply. 'He said once that if more industrialists had as much common sense and compassion as Mr Addison the world would be a much better place.'

'High praise,' retorted Melly with acid emphasis. 'Perhaps his compassion doesn't extend to his personal life, although I think we can agree that his common sense does.'

'Is that what you want from him? Compassion?'

Melly sighed. 'No, of course it's not. I just don't know. I'm afraid I want more than he's capable of giving.'

Sara was completely trustworthy, which was just as well, for Melly had admitted more than was safe. As the men chose that moment to turn back towards the house the subject perforce was changed.

'Look, why don't you stay to lunch?' Sara asked persuasively. 'It's almost time for it. We could have a drink first, and if you aren't doing anything this afternoon it's a lovely day to spend around the pool.'

'I'd love to,' Melly said doubtfully, 'but we'll have to ask Trent. He said something about sailing.'

But Trent was more than happy to eat lunch with the Hornings, so they sat in the shade of an enormous silk tree and drank chilled white wine, then they all trooped into the kitchen and gathered up salads and cold meat and pâté while Sara heated crusty rolls of bread and Jim found the necessary tools to eat with.

There were old trees all around the section, lending the very modern pool and terraces a desirable maturity. Sara hadn't allowed any shortage of money to force her into making rash purchases; Melly sank gratefully into an extremely comfortable chair and watched almost silently as Trent's charm dazzled their hosts.

It was strange, she would not have thought that he and Jim would have much in common, yet they were talking like old friends, a rapid run-through of current events, not too much business and then a quick exploration of sports in which they discovered they both enjoyed sailing.

'What sort of yacht?' Jim asked eagerly.

Trent smiled. 'At the moment I'm between them. I sold *Wave Cleaver* at the end of last season.'

The name meant nothing to Melly, but Jim looked staggered. 'Of course,' he said on a note of self-disgust, 'I knew I should have recognised you. I saw you win the Hundred Miles last year.' He whistled. 'It was like nothing I've ever seen before, I couldn't believe it! She came out of the murk and weather like a ship bound for hell, I'll swear I heard the rigging screaming, and the chap next to me said——'

Trent grinned at his abrupt stop. 'I can guess,' he said drily.

'Yes, well, he was torn between admiration and total astonishment that anything could stay upright in that hurricane. Your gear must have been completely trustworthy. I'm damned if I'd have trusted myself to weather like that in anything other than a destroyer!'

Trent's eyes flicked to Melly's face.

'She came through it without any gear failure,' he said even more drily. 'I'm not as reckless as my reputation, believe me. I trust my crew and I make sure that the boat and the gear is as good as it can be.'

'Then you go hell-for-leather,' said Jim, his voice a blend of satisfaction, and envy and awe. 'Why did you sell her? She's still the fastest thing New Zealand's seen in her class.'

Trent leaned back into his chair, shifting his broad shoulders in a slight, restless movement. Through the filmy leaves of the silk tree a ray of sunlight found its way aslant his face, tiger-striping him so that, for a second, he looked like some primitive warrior made up for war.

Then he moved and the illusion was gone. Lightly he said, 'I'd got what I wanted from her. It was time to move on.'

Jim leaned forward, asking eagerly, 'Have you commissioned a new one?'

'Yes, but nothing like *Wave Cleaver*, I'm going conventional. I want a family boat, something to cruise in. I'm getting too old for thunder and lightning.'

Jim responded to his wry self-deprecation with a disbelieving and rather regretful grin. But Melly, who had been listening, all ears, met Trent's taunting glance with a swift sparkling one of her own. Men! Never satisfied, always testing their limits, recklessly in love with speed and danger.

'Won't you miss the excitement?' Jim asked now.

The broad shoulders lifted in a shrug. 'No,' Trent said flatly, adding with an air of candour which hid malice and mockery, 'I intend to get my excitement from other aspects of my life from now on.'

It was obvious what he meant. Both Sara and Jim noticed the way that pale gaze touched deliberately on Melly's mouth before dropping to the full curve of her breasts. Melly felt the colour crawl along her cheekbones as the Hornings exchanged a quick, knowing look, and her mouth tightened as she flashed a brilliantly black glance sharp with warning at Trent. Don't lay any claim to me, she said without the need for words.

Implacable yet amused, he answered in the same manner, and Melly felt the heat rise from her throat again. For his eyes told her that the claim had already been staked. All he was doing now was publicising it!

He was, she thought grimly, too clever to say anything definite, anything that could be refuted. No, he preferred to hint and use that voice and those eyes to make his meaning explicit. Yet there was nothing she could say to contradict him. Her teeth worried at her lower lip as she stared down at her lap.

After a few minutes of desultory conversation she heard her name and lifted her head.

'Swim?' asked Sara. 'I can lend you a bikini your size.'

Melly hesitated, then said lightly, 'Why not? If I stay here I might just go to sleep.'

The bikini was scarlet and brief, cut so high in the legs that hers seemed to start from her waist, and the bra preserved the barest—literally—minimum of decency.

'Oh, my goodness!' Sara exclaimed, then turned and yelled through the door of the changing room, 'Jim, you shut your eyes!'

'Why?'

Sara laughed. 'Never mind, just you do it.' To Melly

she said, 'You look absolutely superb, like a dark Venus.'

'I can't wear this,' Melly protested, gazing down the long golden length of her body.

'Oh yes, you can. You should wear red, it brings out the passion in you.'

'It's too skimpy.'

'Rubbish,' Sara said robustly, pushing her through the door. 'You look like every man's fantasy. Why so bashful? I thought in the South of France everyone went topless?'

'Yes, but not me, and this thing is practically bottomless as well!' wailed Melly.

'It covers everything that needs to be covered.' Sara herself was dressed in an extremely sketchy bikini, but somehow on her small figure it didn't look so—so *naked*! Nowhere near so much skin, Melly thought confusedly, as they came out into the sunlight.

And there was Jim, standing obediently with his eyes tightly shut, and Trent, who for one incredible moment looked as though he had been granted a vision of beauty beyond imagination.

'There,' purred Sara, removing the hand which had urged Melly on, 'she looks absolutely super, doesn't she, Trent? No, Jim, keep your eyes closed until she gets into the water.'

'Yes, by God.' For once Trent showed his emotions, his expression shaken, one hand lifting in an entirely involuntary movement.

Dimly Melly saw the satisfaction on Sara's vivid little face and was conscious of Jim's presence at the edge of the pool. Dimly the sun glittered on the dark water, dimly the flowers beneath the trees glowed like fluorescent jewels. Her eyes were caught, transfixed by the sight of Trent standing watching her, the sunlight sliding over his magnificent body in great slabs of gold, highlighting the bronze shoulders and the narrow waist, the long, tautly-muscled legs.

As she stood there dry-mouthed, her primary thoughts were a kind of awe mixed with an intolerable pleasure of the eyes. How was it that she had never seen him like this before? He looked, she thought dazedly, beautiful, his lean well-muscled strength emphasised the smooth bronze skin marked by a fine scrollwork of hair that arrowed down beyond the trunks he wore in a message as explicitly sexual as the sudden tightening of her breasts and the heat that sprang into life between her thighs.

The spell of their absorption was broken by Jim's plaintive voice. 'How much longer do I have to stand here with my eyes shut, for heaven's sake? Is Melly decent yet?'

Thickly, his voice barely audible, Trent said, 'For God's sake, Melissa, go and change.'

And, frightened, Melissa did just that, scrambling into a one-piece suit that Sara produced only because she thought that if she refused to swim it would make too much of those bewildering moments when her eyes had met Trent's and the world had faded into a sensual haze.

Now, armoured by a fierce self-control, she listened a moment to the splashing in the pool before once more walking out into the sun.

Sara and Jim were playing together, laughing and spluttering, but Trent was swimming, strong arms dragging him through the water as he went from one end of the pool to the other.

'Well,' said Jim, eyeing her with interest, 'if the other togs were more revealing than that I wish I'd peeked!'

Melly smiled, a mirthless movement of stiff lips, then dived in, carefully choosing an area as far away from Trent's single-minded exercise as possible. Like him she wanted to assuage the savage frustration that gripped her by exhausting herself, but she allowed herself to be inveigled into the Hornings' game, and after a while the ache in her body eased and her laughter lost its forced note.

But Trent still swam alone until after half an hour or so, when whatever demons had been chasing him gave up, he came across to where they all sat on the wide steps.

'No wonder you take your boat out in tempests,' Jim said cheerfully. 'If the damned thing did go down you'd be able to swim ashore!'

Water sheeted from Trent's shoulders and face when he leaned back. He showed no signs of strain, yet his chest rose and fell a couple of times as though his breath was difficult to get. Melly averted her eyes, feeling a return of that dry-mouthed sensation which had accompanied those moments when they had looked at each other and recognised the same primitive elemental attraction.

'I keep fit by swimming,' Trent said. 'I'm not one for team sports, or even those needing a partner.'

'A loner,' Sara nodded wisely.

He grinned. 'I suppose so. Like Melissa. She runs for exercise.'

Something twisted deep inside her. It was dangerously sweet to be coupled with him, even in so mundane a matter.

'What about sailing?' objected Jim. 'That's a team sport, if you like. You have to have a crew.'

'Yes, although I must admit for sheer pleasure I enjoy dinghy racing best, when there's just me. However, I like to go out in bad weather, so a bigger boat is necessary.' Eyes half closed against the glitter of the sun on the water, he stared across the pool, continuing slowly, 'On *Wave Cleaver* I was in charge, I was alone.'

'Your crew must have trusted you implicitly,' Jim commented, looking at him with something like hero-worship.

Trent's brow lifted in amusement and wry acceptance. 'They're just as foolhardy as I am and they knew *Wave Cleaver* had been commissioned for the sort of conditions I like.' Jim acknowledged this with a smile and a nod, but it was obvious that Trent's remark hadn't changed his mind. That respectful awe was still hinted at in his eyes.

The rest of the afternoon passed in lazy contented relaxation; at least, that was how it seemed to affect the others. Melly had to fight to suppress the scintillating little shivers of excitement that ran through her veins instead of the more mundane blood. Whenever Trent's eyes, purposeful as a hunting shark's, ran over the length of her legs or touched on her narrow waist or the ample curves of her breast, the electricity between them was re-charged.

If he had come out with it in the crudest manner he couldn't have made it plainer. There was possession in his gaze, open and blatant, and a satisfaction that made her grit her teeth in fury. Those long moments when they had recognised each other without concealment or restraint had made him supremely confident that he had her.

Well, she thought icily, he'll find out how wrong he is soon enough!

Intent upon her own thoughts, she missed some part of the conversation. A vital part, she realised, when it became clear that Trent had invited the Hornings out to dinner. Naturally they had accepted, although Sara's squeal when Trent mentioned the name of a restaurant was edged with shock.

'Celebrating something?' asked Jim with the absorbed look of a man who is trying to work out whether he can afford something.

Trent grinned, that wolfish slash which suggested the untamed power of the man. Laughter gleamed in the depths of his eyes as he flicked a glance towards Melly.

'Yes,' he said simply, leaving her in no doubt that it was her capitulátion he meant. 'You'll be my guests, of course.'

'But will you be able to get in?' Sara stammered a little, her open expression revealing that for a while she had forgotten who he was. 'I believe you have to reserve *months* ahead.'

Trent said cynically, 'The law of the market places still operates, even with fashionable restaurants. May I use your telephone?'

'Yes, of course.' Jim took him inside, leaving Sara to gaze a little unhappily at Melly.

'Put my foot into it, didn't I? No, don't tell me I didn't. It was just that—he's so *nice*, I forgot that he's a tycoon.'

'Well, I don't suppose he has much difficulty in buying anything he needs—or wants,' said Melly, her soft, deep voice every bit as cynical as Trent's had been.

'But not you,' Sara said quickly, thoughtfully.

Melly looked her appreciation, aware that the smile was tinged with bitterness yet unable to conceal it. 'No,' she said quietly.

'He's in love with you.' Sara spoke with complete confidence. 'I've seen it. It's there when he watches you.'

'Greedily? Yes, I know. If you can call it love. He was in love with me when he married Cathy. Some *love*!'

Very wisely Sara said, 'You always did set impossibly high standards for those you loved. I suppose it comes from having a brother who's a paragon.'

Melly snorted with laughter. 'Oh, Rafe may look like a dark angel, but he doesn't behave like one, believe me. For one thing, he's got the devil's own temper.'

'You idolised him when you were a kid. I suppose you view all men with an eye to how they measure up against him. But Mel,' Sara leaned forward to make her point, her small face earnest, 'you can't assess one man

against another as if they were—well, works of art, or
bottles of wine! And for what it's worth, I think you'd
better get used to the idea of being Mrs Trent Addison,
because I'll bet there's precious little he wants that he
doesn't get. He's tough and he's determined and he's
probably ruthless, and he wants you!'

She finished hurriedly, for the men were on their way
back. As she sat back into her chair she asked
cheerfully, 'All organised?'

It was a needless question, they all knew, but Trent
answered it. 'Yes. We'll pick you up at eight. How does
that sound?'

'Fine. Oh,' Sara was girlishly enthusiastic, 'I am
excited! I'll wear my most beautiful dress and stun
everyone with my allure!'

Trent looked down at her with amused appreciation.
'I can hardly wait,' he said, 'but I'll bet you don't look
any more beautiful than you do now.'

Sara's blush was deep, her answering smile spontan-
eous. 'Comments like that could turn my head,' she
told him, fluttering her lashes flirtatiously in a parody
of amorousness that set them all laughing.

Even Melly laughed, although to do it she had to
subdue a lancing, acid pain which horrified her by its
ferocity. Jealousy, she thought numbly.

It went, of course, there was no need for it, Sara and
Trent were only teasing each other, yet the fact that she
could feel such pain over so trivial an incident appalled
Melly and kept her more silent than was usual on the
way home.

'Tired?' Trent asked gently.

She shook her head, then changed her mind and said,
'A little, I suppose.'

He chuckled. 'I'd expected a tirade all the way home
on my perfidy!'

'It would be wasted effort,' she retorted crisply.

'I'm glad you've realised that it's futile to resist.' His

hand covered hers, warm and strong, the fingers entwining with hers. He squeezed, then lifted their linked hands and set hers on his thigh.

Melly flinched at the solid sheet of muscle beneath her fingers, remembering those moments by the pool when he had looked like a god from an ancient tale, triumphant in his virile masculinity.

As if her hand had been seared by unbearable heat she jerked it back on to her own lap, closing her ears to his satisfied chuckle.

Oh, he was clever. Sara was right in her summing up of his character; he was everything she had said, tough and merciless, determined on his own way. He had used Sara and Jim, invited them out to dinner because he knew that Melly would have refused any more invitations from him. He had made it impossible for her to object, but this time, she decided, would be the last. Never again.

She wore dull purple, a colour which should have made her dowagerish, but which combined with the pale gold of her skin and her black eyes and hair to create a vital, flaunting creature of the night. The silk jersey clung lovingly to her breasts and hips, and swirled with insolent elegance about her legs, pointing up their length and grace.

Old amethysts glittered in her ears and a large stone surrounded by diamonds graced her finger. Slowly, carefully, she coloured her mouth a rich ripe scarlet, thanking the Hollingworth genes which enabled her to get away with a certain amount of drama. A mist of perfume, exotic and oriental, and she was ready, anticipation beating high in her throat.

Trent gave her a long, intent look, before asking with dangerous lightness, 'Going out with all flags flying, Melissa?'

And he gave a feral smile at the startled involuntary response, the indrawn breath and swift glance upwards from beneath her lashes.

'Struggle all you like,' he told her laconically, 'it will get you nowhere.'

She had nothing to say to that; no word was spoken until they reached the Hornings'. Then courtesy brought Melly's manners to the fore; she responded to Sara's transparent delight with what she hoped appeared to be high spirits and from then on the evening took off.

The restaurant was fashionable, but it was good, too, the atmosphere gracious and friendly, the service unobtrusively excellent, the food and wine list sophisticated and superb.

For Sara it was all enhanced by the fact that she recognised several celebrities, including one American pop star whose love life was X-rated.

'I can see why,' Sara hissed, 'he's gorgeous looking, isn't he? I wonder why he hasn't got his latest—that Italian contessa—with him. I thought they were inseparable. Hey, Mel, he's giving you the eye!' She had drunk enough of the wine to make her a little reckless; her eyes glittered with laughter and speculation as she leaned towards Melly. 'Yes, he's definitely looking our way. Gosh, he's really something! All that brooding passion directed right at you, Mel.'

'Nonsense.' Melly didn't even look towards the table where the singer was seated. She was too conscious of the smile on Trent's face and the hint of violence it expressed to be bothered with any pop star, however brooding and sexy.

Sara giggled. 'No, truly, he's been watching you for quite a while. I wonder if all the stories you read about him are true.'

'Couldn't possibly be.' Melly's voice was calm and assured, lightened with a little mockery. 'No man could have that much stamina.'

'Publicity,' Jim agreed, frowning at his ebullient wife. He was afraid she would offend Trent Addison; his apprehension showed in his face.

Melly suddenly felt sick. Why should Sara, who was bright and bubbling and often a little thoughtless, but oh, so kind, so completely free from malice, be put in this position because Trent was powerful? Jim should be ashamed of himself for his lack of loyalty, she thought as she threw a scornful glance at him, and an even more glittering one at the man beside her.

He was looking down into his wine glass, the long sensitive fingers caressing the stem with sensuous tactile enjoyment. Just so had they smoothed over her skin, openly enjoying its smoothness and warmth. A slow heat began to feed through Melly's body as she remembered.

As if he felt her glare Trent lifted his head, the wide, thin mouth curved in a smile that had no humour in it. Instead there was a wry resignation that bewildered her until she understood it. Then the fierce anger that flamed in her dark gaze fled. She suddenly felt an immense sympathy for him, able for the first time to appreciate how a man might sell his honour for power and then discover how bitter a bargain he had made.

Warned by Jim's frown, Sara had subsided into silence, her expressive face now concerned.

Trent smiled at her, warmly, rather teasingly, as though she was a much loved and indulged younger sister. 'Would you like to meet him?' he asked gently.

Sara's eyes rounded with astonishment. 'Truly?'

'Oh, yes.' He sounded a little weary, his eyes half closed so that the glance which roved Melly's face was enigmatic. 'I've had dealings with him and we've met several times.'

'Gosh!' Sara smiled her excitement as Trent signalled a waiter and sent a note across the room.

As if it had been a signal the pop star and his entourage of three men nodded across the intervening space. The man who Trent said was his manager spoke to the waiter, who sped off to the maître d'hôtel. There was a subdued conference.

'What's happening?' asked Sara, agog.

Trent gave her a sardonic smile. 'Face-saving. He won't come to our table because that would look as though I'd summoned him. So they'll organise a table big enough to take all of us.'

'But this place is incredibly discreet.'

'And by tomorrow morning everyone in Auckland who's interested, and quite a few who couldn't care less, will know exactly what happened.'

The waiter approached, smiling, eager. Within a few seconds they had all been transferred to the second table, and introductions had been performed all round. There was a lot of smiling and shaking of hands and when they sat down Melly was not really surprised to find Trent on one side of her and the pop singer, whose name was Ryk Ward, on the other, because he was making no attempt to disguise the fact that he fancied her.

Weird, she thought, as she listened to him telling her about the concert he was to give the following night. Now if she had been Jennet, her half-sister, she could have understood it because Jennet was possessed of a rare, exotic beauty which was a seduction in itself. Men were instantly attracted to Jennet.

But not, normally, to Melly, whose height tended to be intimidating and whose features were too severe to be either fashionable or beautiful.

Yet Ryk Ward's blue eyes were heated and openly desirous as they roamed her face and she could feel some strong emotion beneath the brooding façade he presented.

It was only a façade, too, although a deceiving one. He was amusing, a little arrogant, enjoying Sara's ingenuous delight in the evening with a calm acceptance which should have irritated Melly, but didn't. Ryk Ward knew very well that he was one of the beautiful people; he showed no signs of conceit, but he knew his own worth.

And although he flirted charmingly with Sara it was to Melly that his interest was directed. She remembered reading somewhere that he steered strictly clear of married women. Bemused, but with caution never far from the surface, she responded politely to his charm, ignoring as well as she was able the burning looks and the smiles he sent her way.

She was eating mango soufflé and Trent was engaged in a low-voiced conversation with the manager when Ryk Ward's hand dropped over hers, rested there for a deliberate moment and then was removed.

She met the blandly enquiring look on his face with a winged lift of her brows.

'I'm not getting anywhere, am I,' he stated.

'Sorry.'

He grinned. 'Thought it was too good to be true!'

Melly's brows climbed further. He leaned closer, saying almost below his breath, 'I thought you were bait, darling! Your man there has been setting up a deal with my agent; it wouldn't be the first time a pretty girl's been used as a sweetener. And he knew I was coming here this evening.'

Melly bit her lip, colour leaving her cheeks. 'Well, I can assure you it's not the case this time,' she snapped back *sotto voce*, adding without thinking, 'I'm sure Trent doesn't work that way.'

'Oh, you'd be surprised what people will do when it comes to money,' he said, so profoundly cynical that her indignant outcry died stillborn.

Money—and power. An incredible suspicion struck her and she glanced at Trent's toughly-defined profile, the hawk nose and stark line of the jaw, the tanned skin stretched over a bone structure of chiselled strength. He must have felt her stare, for he turned his head and met her eyes, his own quizzical, almost taunting.

Surely not! Oh, please God, surely not. If she hadn't realised just how much her subconscious had been hoping she knew it now because the ugly suspicion was like a blow to her heart. She tore her gaze away, aware that Ryk Ward was still watching her, his dark eyes as hard in their way as Trent's gaze.

The spoon in the dish before her wavered. *No*, she could not cry, not here, not now. Fiercely she blinked, then swallowed.

'Perhaps,' she said, and her voice was almost even, almost light. 'Fortunately I don't move in circles where that sort of amoral behaviour is the norm.'

Was that pity in Ryk's dark gaze? Trent had turned back to his discussion, but she felt the weight of his attention as though he had some sixth sense which was monitoring the conversation.

'Good for you,' said Ryk Ward, adding not unsympathetically, 'Mind you, it happens everywhere. At your man's level the stakes are higher, that's the only difference.'

'I'd hate to be as cynical as you!'

He smiled, and yes, there was pity there, and a kind of tired acceptance. 'Oh, I spent the first twenty-two years of my life trusting people. Then I woke up one morning and found myself famous and bankrupt. My manager, ably aided by my own stupid naïvety, had milked me of everything he could, and that was about everything. I got back what I could, which wasn't much, and since then I've made sure no one else has ripped me off. Your man will tell you, people who trust are fools.'

'He's not my man,' Melly said angrily, suddenly exhausted.

His answering chuckle was disbelieving. 'You're in love with him—I can tell. Won't he play ball? Get what you can out of him, darlin', and then leave him before he boots you out. That way you'll keep some pride. Men are rats, even the best of us.'

As if the words had been a signal—although he

couldn't possibly have heard—Trent turned away from his low-voiced discussion with Ryk's manager to say coolly, 'Has your appetite gone, Melissa? I'll get that removed——'

'No,' she said, picking up the spoon again. Across the table Sara laughed at something the third man in Ryk's entourage said to her. The gay open sound made Melly feel immensely old, stripped of all her illusions.

After that the evening was a nightmare. Sara and Jim were obviously enjoying themselves, even Ryk and his cohorts had relaxed and were happily widening Sara's eyes with tales of their world, some ribald, some shocking, all entertaining. Melly forced herself to join in, all the time acutely sensitive to Trent's nearness beside her, by word and look and gesture staking a claim to her that was subtle but impossible to miss. It was such a contrast to his earlier attitude that she couldn't prevent herself from wondering if he had indeed intended to use her to charm Ryk Ward. It was not possible, her heart told her, Trent was a possessive man who would not share, but into her brain there came the recollection of an article she had read somewhere, pointing out that Ryk Ward's girl-friends all conformed to a certain physical type; they were, she remembered sickly, all tall, with full breasts and dark hair and eyes.

The mere thought of such depravity on Trent's part tore her apart. She could not deal with it here, not in any constructive way, so she forced it away from her conscious mind and set herself out to be as charming and pleasant as she could.

Her relief when the evening was over was short-lived. In the car the hideous conjectures crawled back to take over her brain, obscene, sickening her into silence and introspection.

'Lord, I'm tired!' Sara smothered a yawn. 'Oh, that was fun, I did enjoy it so much, thank you, Trent.'

'I'm so glad,' he said suavely.

Sara asked them in for coffee, but Trent refused, using Melly's tiredness as an excuse.

'I'll ring you,' Sara told her. 'Good night—good night, Trent.'

It took a tense few minutes for him to negotiate the silent roads back to The Towers. Melly stared defiantly out of the window, her weary eyes held open by willpower alone. Soon it would be Christmas and she would go up to Te Puriri and forget Trent while she was there. And afterwards she would make some excuse and find herself a flat with several other girls who would be some kind of protection against him if he ever came to call. When she had done that she would look around for another job, because she couldn't go on like this.

She knew now that the love she had thought dead was still very much alive; like a plant in the desert it had gone underground when deprived of nourishment, but it had only taken Trent's presence to revivify it.

Well, so what? It just proved that she was an idiot. Perhaps it ran in the family. Rafe and Jennet had loved each other for years before events conspired to throw them into such close proximity that they were forced to face the issue. They had been lucky; there was likely to be no such happy ending for her.

CHAPTER SEVEN

OUTSIDE her door Trent looked into her face, holding her chin so that she could not avoid his unsparing assessment.

'You look exhausted,' he said roughly.

Melly's smooth shoulders moved in the slightest of shrugs while her breath caught in her throat.

'All in a good cause, I believe,' she said with crisp derision.

His black brows drew together. 'And what exactly do you mean by that?'

'Well, our little outing turned out to be rather profitable for you, didn't it?'

'Oh yes.' His mouth hardened, then he said, 'You've got great shadows under your eyes and although I can see you're spoiling for a fight I'm not going to indulge you now. I'll see you in the morning.'

'I'm going out.'

He didn't believe her, that was certain, but he said, 'Right, I'll take you. What time?'

'Nine forty-five,' she bit back.

He laughed beneath his breath and bent his head. On her eyelids his mouth was warm and gentle, but she could feel the heat radiating from his taut body, and knew that his control was tenuous.

'Good night,' he whispered, and brought his mouth down on hers in a kiss as seducingly sweet as the sensations radiating from it throughout her body. As deceitful as moonlight on quicksands.

It was easy enough to sleep. Before she removed her make-up Melly took one of a packet of sleeping pills she found in the cabinet and by the time she was ready for bed she was already yawning.

It was the telephone that woke her, its impatient ring sawing through a brain which seemed strangely woolly and lethargic.

'Yes?' she muttered into the receiver.

'What on earth's the matter with you? I've been trying to get you for five minutes! I was just on my way down——'

'I'm sorry, I slept in,' she said, stifling a yawn as she dragged herself up on to the pillows. Her hand moved to her forehead as she tried to massage away the incipient throbbing behind it.

'You did, indeed. It's now nine-thirty. Do you still want to go to church?'

'How did you know that was where——' She stopped, angry because she had given herself away.

The tormenting note of mockery was very evident. 'I can read your mind,' Trent said drily.

Melly sighed. 'Yes, I can be ready on time. It's only five minutes' walk.'

The calm and peace of the service drove away her needling headache and left her feeling almost restored. But even for a restful night she wasn't ever going to try sleeping pills again, she thought gloomily as Trent escorted her across the road. They left you feeling like yesterday's porridge.

She intended going straight to her apartment, but Trent pressed the button for his own—there were other people in the lift, so she contented herself with a speaking glance at him and then kept her head turned rigidly away. Unfortunately this provided her with an excellent view of two women who were coyly watching him from beneath fluttering, flirting lashes.

Sharks! she thought unfairly. Making idiots of themselves. The last of them got off at Melly's floor, but as she made to follow, Trent's fingers tangled in the soft heavy tresses at the nape of her neck and by the time she had told him what she thought of such a cavalier way of restraining her they had stopped on the top floor and he was urging her out, his smile superbly sardonic.

Oh Lord, she thought, panic-stricken. Oh Lord, I love him so!

He gave her breakfast at a table on the terrace beneath the satyr's knowing gaze, champagne and freshly squeezed orange juice followed by scrambled eggs flecked with fresh herbs and topped with caviar, delectable whole-grain toast and croissants spiced with several exotic jams.

'Where did you learn to cook like this?' she asked, her stomach telling her in no uncertain terms that it was well past her normal breakfast time. 'It's superb. Usually I just have yoghurt.'

'I know. I don't have a particularly wide repertoire, but what I do, I do well.'

She nodded. 'Oh, you do indeed!'

Afterwards he ate strawberries while she sipped tea and watched the desultory Sunday life of the suburbs pass beneath them, her nerves stretching unbearably. She knew that he was biding his time, that he intended to finish the quarrel she had tried to start last night. There was a kind of hard decision about him now as he watched her across the table and his eyes had splintered into quartz.

Trust him to conduct a quarrel on his own terms, in his own apartment and at the time of his choosing!

Yet he was not going to have it all his own way. Unconsciously belligerent, Melly's glance snapped a warning over the rim of her tea-cup.

'See how considerate I can be,' he said with a grim little smile. 'I got you up in time to make your peace with your Maker, then fed you so that your brain isn't starved of nourishment . . .'

She shifted uneasily in her chair, lowering her cup to the table, her eyes dropping to note the way the sun gleamed in the clear amber liquid like a small gold coin. For a moment she wanted nothing more than to surrender, to tell him that she would marry him. It would be so easy to give in, so natural.

Yet she could not. Once she married—if she married—she would be committed to him for ever. If he betrayed her—and there were so many treacheries which could happen in a marriage—he would tear her heart out. Self-preservation, plain and selfish, brought her chin up so that she met his menacing gaze with one, frigid, in return.

'Now,' he said silkily, 'just exactly what did Ryk Ward say to you that made you go dumb and stubborn last night?'

Remembered anguish trembled across her lips, but she firmed them, saying 'I'm sorry, I hoped no one noticed.'

'Well, he did, but he doesn't count. Your friends were enjoying themselves too much to see. What was it, my heart's lady?'

'He thought you were using me as bait.' In the singing sunlight the words came out bald and ugly, as crude as the unpleasant suspicion Ryk had planted in her brain.

Brief colour flecked her cheeks, but she made herself watch him, search for some hint, some clue to what he was thinking. The cold grey eyes held hers, totally lacking in emotion. I'll bet he's a super poker player, she thought almost hysterically.

'And you believed him?' Trent asked evenly.

She bit her lip, then said with trenchant emotion, 'No—oh, how should I know? You certainly didn't lay any claims to me until after it must have been obvious that I wasn't prepared to play along.'

'You did believe him.'

Pitilessly his eyes lanced across her face, making her flush with guilt, and self-contempt because it was guilt she felt instead of righteous indignation.

'Just for the record,' said Trent, icily polite, 'I didn't lay claims, as you put it, because you've more than made your feelings on that particular issue obvious, and I wanted both you and your friends to enjoy the evening without any tantrums from you. So I was on my best behaviour until Ward made a pass at you. As we're likely to be seeing something of him in the future I wasn't going to have him think you were available. He's a lecherous swine and unfortunately, so his manager told me, you fit in very well with his ideal of feminine desirability.'

The strong bones of her face sharpened beneath a suddenly sallow skin. Nervously she ran her tongue along her bottom lip, unaware that she was looking imploringly at him.

But even as she was saying, 'I'm sorry,' he muttered, 'Oh, what the hell! You don't believe me, do you? To you I'm the pirate you despise, someone who snatches what he wants without caring who gets hurt in the process.'

Indignation stiffened her, the apologies drying up on her tongue. 'Yes,' she said defiantly. 'If you weren't, you'd have explained—you'd tell me why you—you——'

'Dumped you? Jilted you?' his laughter was harsh, frightening. 'If I said I had no alternative, would you believe me?'

'Yes,' she said acidly, 'because marriage to Cathy was the only way you could get control of Sir Peter's interests. Obviously you had no alternative. After all, it's power that turns you on, isn't it? When you made love to her did you close your eyes and visualise all that money and power . . .' She stopped, appalled at the savage jealousy that had forced that vulgarity from her, her eyes jerking up to meet his in tormented apprehension.

Trent's face was pale, expressionless until he looked

directly at her. Then she could see the whiter line around his mouth and the flaming ice that was his gaze, and she was frightened as she had never been before in her life. This was a Trent she had never seen, never known existed, the civilised mask torn from his face to expose the destructive forces behind.

'I never touched her,' he said, so low she had to strain to hear him, his thin lips barely moving.

Anger was the only protection she had against the fire-storm of emotion she had evoked. Linking her trembling hands together in her lap, she said defiantly, 'Why should you? You'd got what you wanted, hadn't you? I don't suppose it worried you in the least to cheat her even further. Or didn't she want you, either?'

'What I wanted,' he said in that dreadful toneless voice, 'was you. And now I have you—now I'm going to have you.'

For a moment she thought she had misheard him, but one glance at his face disabused her of that. He was watching her with naked, unabated lust, his expression set in lines of bitterness and determination. He looked like a hunter who was about to kill prey he both hated and coveted.

Subduing her instinct to flee in panic because instinct told her that if she did she would be doomed, Melly opened her mouth to speak.

And only then did she realise how terrified she was, for her vocal chords refused to work. All the clasping in the world could not stop the shaking of her hands across her thighs; she felt a disgusting sensation in her stomach. Fear, stripped of all accoutrements but the raw powerful need to flee.

'Trent,' her lips shaped as he came towards her, blocking out the sun, and he smiled and curved his hand around the nape of her neck.

'I've waited too long,' he murmured. 'Appetites too long suppressed become obsessions, and obsessed men are dangerous, Melissa. I'm going to have you.'

'No!' It was a choked little syllable and her voice broke halfway through as she tried to ward him off with hands she couldn't even clench, they were so nerveless. Incredibly she remembered how he had held her hand and made it into a fist that first day they had seen each other again. This had been inevitable, even then.

Relentlessly he pulled her to her feet, that bitter smile still curving his mouth. 'Yes,' he whispered, pulling her into him so that she felt the hard aroused tension of his body. 'Yes, my dearest love.'

His mouth on hers was a brand, searing away everything but a primitive response at that most basic of levels, man to woman, male to female; Melly moaned, her brain shutting off as she felt the rise of a slow, mindless, inexorable response in every cell of her body.

'This is rape,' she whispered. His hand in the curls at the nape of her neck tilted her head back so that the taut, satiny arc of her neck was presented to his desperate lips.

Trent said nothing, but his arm across her back tightened. Each pressure point jolted into wrenching awareness, like a million tiny electric shocks in her body. The potent masculine odour brought a shudder of delight to some primitive part of her. His mouth on her throat was hot and seeking; she trembled as his tongue left a scant trail of moisture down its length, trembled again as it stopped over the hollow where a frantically beating pulse shouted its message of arousal and hunger. It seemed that several layers of skin had been stripped away, leaving her so sensitive to his touch that it was a tormenting ecstasy.

A flood of heat suffused her body, originating in that arch-betrayer, the pit of her stomach, surging unresisted to her limbs and her face and her breasts, crushed now against the hard width of his chest.

Dizzily, barely able to articulate, she said thickly, 'If you loved me you wouldn't do this to me, Trent. You couldn't!'

It was the only weapon she could think of to use against him; it was a course of desperation. The battle was almost over, the fortress lost through treachery from within, and he knew it, he had experience enough to read all of the signs and portents.

'It's too late for that,' he whispered deeply against the hollow at the base of her throat. 'Too late, Melissa. It's not the way I want it, but if this is the only way I can get you—so be it.'

He took her mouth again, forcing it to open beneath his, and in the face of his determined assault she surrendered, racked by a hunger to match his, all thought of resistance fled from a brain which existed now only to register the message her senses brought it, the tensile pleasure of bone and muscle and skin like silk as her hands slipped beneath his shirt to caress his back and pull him even closer to her.

The taste of him in her mouth was salty, masculine. For some reason—some coward's reason—she clamped her eyes shut, appreciating him through her other senses, her body singing with an urgent joy which could no longer be suppressed. She felt strong, buoyed by desire, and weak, shaking with erotic unknown sensations as his hands slid the dress from her shoulders to fall in a whispering heap about her feet.

'Oh Melly,' he muttered harshly, 'you are so exquisite!'

Later Melly would wonder why the possiblity of being seen hadn't occurred to her; at that moment, inflamed with the heat of his hands on her body, she couldn't have cared less.

Later she would appreciate just how skilled a lover he was, using his hands and his mouth and a vast knowledge of feminine sensuality to woo her along the path he wanted her to take, advancing slowly yet purposefully, so that even when he picked her up and took her through the glass doors into his bedroom she was too lost in the sensual enchantment he had created for the spell to be broken.

Her eyes glowed like slumbrous jewels, her skin was flushed and slightly damp as he unwittingly revealed his strength by yanking back the covers before lowering her on to the sheet. For a moment the haze about her seemed to dissipate; she stared around blankly, but his head came down, the heat and dampness of his mouth enclosed the tip of her breast and her body jerked in a spasm of exquisite feeling.

'So beautifully eager,' he said beneath his breath, keeping his mouth there until he had undone the catch of her bra. Lovingly, his eyes ablaze, he freed her from the lace garment before lifting his head to feast on the riches he had exposed.

No longer in the least shy, Melly watched through half-closed eyes as his hand cupped her breast. Against the pale gold of her skin his fingers were dark, hardness against softness, masculine strength against the more subtle, more dangerous power which her femininity gave her.

Yet beside the desire that flushed his features, there was awe and tenderness, and his strong hand shook as it traced the curves of her body, the narrow span of her waist, the feminine contour of hips and stomach, the silken skin of thighs and shoulders and throat.

'It's been so long,' he said thickly against her mouth. 'So long, my darling girl . . .'

She didn't know what he meant, she didn't care. She was too busy sliding his shirt away from his shoulders, her eyes as hungry as his as they devoured the raw potency of the body she was freeing. Just as he explored hers, her hands traced across the width of his shoulders, the pads of her fingers revelling in the shift and play of the muscles beneath the smooth, heated skin. Absorbed, rapt, she followed the path of the scrolls of hair across his chest until his stomach tightened beneath her hands and she looked up into his face and smiled.

How could she know what she looked like? Slightly swollen mouth, eyes which were soft and sleepy and avid, the high flush of passion along her cheekbones; Trent groaned and brought his head down, forcing hers back into the pillows in a kiss that shouted of his overpowering need. Still smiling, she fumbled with the unfamiliar clasp of his belt; he rolled over and removed the rest of his clothes and then took from her the small scrap of silk and lace which was her only covering.

Heat enveloped her at the scorching intensity of his scrutiny. Until then he had been almost restrained. Now, as if the sight of her against the sheets of his bed was the fuse that detonated an explosion, he muttered something unintelligible and took her without further preamble, the driving thrust of his body out of control.

Momentarily it hurt, that barbaric intrusion of all that was masculine in him, but Melly responded in a rhythm as old as the species, as basic as laughter and tears, and the pain was soon gone, the quick involuntary flinch she gave immediately forgotten in the sensations that followed. She was enveloped in heat, her untutored body instinctively adjusting to the force of Trent's masculine demands, her brain monitoring only the sensations it received, the singing tension in her blood, the aching frenzy which made her tighten every muscle in her body, demanding a fulfilment she knew must exist.

Trent's breathing was painful in her ears; through the tumult and the thunder of sensation she could hear his voice, impeded and incoherent. His face looked like a mask, rigid, molten with a hunger too intolerable to be borne. Her eyes closed; she cried out, and what she had been striving for came in a wave of unbelievable pleasure that deafened and blinded her to everything

but her own reactions, turning her inwards on herself so
that she barely sensed the tremors that shook him, then
the complete collapse of the lean, powerful body which
had forced that unbearable ravishment of every one of
her senses.

Perhaps she fainted. Perhaps she slept. When her
overloaded brain returned to something like full
consciousness it was to the realisation that the heavy
thump-thump in her head was the sound of Trent's
heart. She was lying with her head on his shoulder, her
body boneless and silken with pleasure, one hand on
the flat hard plane of his stomach.

And slowly, as muddy water from a flooded stream
taints a river, her mood of sybaritic contentment, that
total relaxation after surrender, changed. Shame
darkened her eyes, mixed with a bitter anger at herself
for responding like—like a woman in love, she told
herself savagely.

Uncannily he echoed her thoughts, saying quietly,
'Now tell me you don't love me.'

It hurt to clear her throat and say harshly, 'It was
only sex.'

'*Only* sex?' Trent laughed sardonically. 'It wasn't *only*
anything, stupid woman. If that was only sex I could
get exactly the same experience from a woman I paid to
sleep with me, and any man who looked at you with
lust could make you feel like that. Do you think Ryk
Ward could have made you respond so wantonly?'

He felt the quick shiver that tightened her skin. His
knowledge of her distaste was clear in his voice as he
went on mercilessly, 'At least you don't try to lie. Why
did you let me think there had been other men for you?'

Melly felt drained; she wanted to lie with his body
warm and hard against hers, his arm around her
shoulder, for the rest of her life.

Aloud she said, 'Does it matter? Would you have left
me alone if you'd known I was a virgin?'

He considered this for several stretched seconds, finally saying, 'No. No, I haven't got superhuman control. I want you too much. But I could have been— gentler. You might have enjoyed it more.'

Almost she laughed. 'I couldn't——' Then she stopped. How could she enjoy anything more than that fire-storm of sensation, the incandescent satisfaction of needs and desires she hadn't even known she possessed?

As for his self-control—he must be possessed of extremely rigid restraint if he had denied himself Cathy Durrant's voluptuous body. Surprisingly in spite of her mother's cynical attitude, she did not doubt him. She knew the strength of his will.

There was laughter and a lazy note of satisfaction in his voice as he said, 'I'm glad it was good for you. Sometimes it isn't, the first time, I wasn't as gentle as I could have been. I've always known there was a whirlwind of passion beneath that rather severe façade you like to present to the world.'

She bit her lip. Wearily, so dispassionately that it was impossible to discern any interest in her voice, she asked, 'How long?'

'Since about a month after I first met you.'

She didn't believe him. She couldn't, and her surprise jerked her head up so that she could look down into his face.

'What?'

He smiled, the bone-deep tiredness she hadn't until then recognised smoothed away as if by a miracle. Somehow, in spite of the fact that he was just as sated as she was, he looked as though he had been revivified.

'Don't you believe me? It's true, I assure you. When we met I was escorting a very—worldly—woman. Within a short time, a very short time, her appeal as a lover faded. A month after I'd met you we agreed to become friends, no more. Since then there's been no one.'

Melly met his clear amused, self-derisive smile with astonishment.

'Don't you believe me?' he asked softly, his hand sliding from her shoulder to follow the long curve of her spine.

It was impossible that she should be aroused. She was exhausted, every scrap of sensuality wrung out of her by his fierce possession. Yet the light touch of his forefinger sent hot little messages along nerves which had never existed until today.

'Yes,' she mumbled, trying to pull away.

Instantly he clamped her against him, pushing her face into his throat. 'No, you don't,' he said harshly. 'You're where you belong, and that's where you're staying until I choose to release you. If it takes me bloody months of taking you, I'll make you admit that you love me.'

His arrogance fired anger in her. 'What about you?' she demanded fiercely.

'What about me?'

'I suppose I'm to love you while you throw me the scraps of emotion you've got left over from being a tycoon. It's the hunt that fascinates you, isn't it, tracking down your quarry? If I lose my head again and fall for you, what happens then?'

'Oh, God!' Trent gave the words that peculiarly masculine tone of aggrieved anger. 'Are you by any chance asking me if I love you? You stupid little bitch, of course I do. I worship the ground you walk on! I always have. When I look at you I feel myself dissipate into weakness, my bones melt, my sinews turn to elastic. Melissa, I——' He turned his head so that his lips touched her hair. 'How can I tell you?' he asked despairingly. 'You're all that I've ever wanted.'

For a moment she believed him. He certainly sounded as though he meant it; there was a ragged note in his voice that caught at her heart. But only for a moment.

Fiercely she retorted, 'It sounds good, Trent, but you forget that you told me that—or much the same as that—three years ago, the night before you put me on the plane to the South of France. A month later I was reading a letter from you which said that you hoped I hadn't read too much into a declaration made in the heat of the moment.'

Melly thought her anger hid the desolation she had felt when she read those cold, excoriating words, but he groaned, 'Hell, I remember, did you really think I'd forgotten? I hoped you'd find—no, damn it, I was overtaken by a fit of nobility; I didn't hope you'd find another love, how could I, the idea clawed at my guts, but I thought I should give you the chance. I wrote exactly the sort of letter I thought would make you hate me.'

'It did that,' she said harshly. One part of her wondered how she could lie with him like this, her cheek crushed into the fine percale pillow, her lips against the slightly rough skin of his throat, enveloped in the warmth from his body. She was imprisoned not only by his lean strength but by the virile aura which enveloped him. It clung to her too, rousing her from the sensual satisfaction she had experienced, taunting her with the knowledge of her frailty where he was concerned.

'My dearest heart, you believed me when I told you that I hadn't made love since I met you. Why can't you believe me in this?'

'Because you haven't *told* me anything!' she wailed before she was able to stop herself.

His hand moved caressingly up her back, seeking the fine arc of her shoulder blades, touching with tactile sensuality the vulnerable nape of her neck beneath the damp curls. Melly shivered at the erotic languor of his touch, her bones melting into honey as the pain and anger and determination dissolved into a slow, golden hunger.

'Don't do that,' she said, almost sobbing. 'I can't think when you touch me. Why *won't* you tell me?'

'Because you won't believe me,' he whispered, turning to meet her so she realised that while he had been tormenting her with his touch her nearness had worked a similar magic on him.

'No!' she gasped, levering herself upward in a flurry of activity. 'I won't let you seduce me into trusting you! I'm not so stupid any more!'

He laughed, his expression coldly amused. 'Then you'll have to decide to love me without the seduction, because I want you, your heart and your brain and this nubile, passionate body and this violence of response, and I don't care how I get it. You belong to me, Melissa, every part of you.'

When she tried to wrench free, long-fingered hands caught her about the waist and lifted her on to him. She gave a strangled gasp—and then the telephone rang, insistent, shocking in the heated atmosphere, so that Trent swore, crudely and desperately, holding her locked to the hard length of his body while he answered it.

'Who—oh! Yes. Yes.' He frowned, then said in a resigned, faintly indulgent voice, 'You're sure now? No hysteria?'

It was a woman. At the sound of the quick, demanding voice Melly stiffened, jealousy ripping its barbs through the body which only a moment ago had been fired with desire.

'Very well,' Trent said now, 'I'll be with you in a few minutes.'

His strong hand replaced the receiver with a little crash. For several moments he lay staring at the ceiling. It hurt to sense the heated passion draining from his body; the pain impelled her to ask in a flat voice,

'Cathy?'

'Cathy,' he said on a half sigh. 'Her grandmother is ill and she's panicking.'

'So she calls you and you go running.' She felt smirched, cheap, as though his ex-wife had prior claims to him and was exercising her rights to prove how little Melly meant in his life. The fact that her emotions were completely illogical did not invalidate them or make them less hard to bear.

'She's only twenty-one,' he said mildly. 'Not a very mature twenty-one, at that. And there's no one else, Melissa.'

'She must be completely alone if she has to rely on the man who *used* her and then discarded her!' Horrified, she cringed at the viciousness in her voice, but her shock did not prevent her from a further taunt, 'Or do you still have to keep on her good side? Did Sir Peter very sensibly make sure that she has some power still?'

His hands came up to frame her face and for a moment she cowered at the fury in his face and his grasp. And then he smiled, a twisted, rather weary smile, and lifted his head from the pillow and kissed her pale lips, those shrewd eyes seeing beneath the anger to the anguish and the uncertainty.

'No,' he said quietly. 'I've complete control of Sir Peter's holdings. Cathy's fortune is like yours, held in trust for her. I'm only one of the trustees. There's nothing she can do to unseat me. But she's alone, Melissa, more alone than you have ever been. Her grandmother is the only person in this world she loves, the only person who has ever loved her unselfishly. Cathy clings to her, and to me, because she's terrified that she'll be left even more alone. Can't you understand that? You've always had the security and love of your family. Is it too much to ask that you have some sympathy for a girl who's been so indulged and spoiled and neglected that her values and feelings of self-worth are about as shaky as a tankstand in an earthquake?'

Melly felt small and thoughtless and nasty, her bitter jealousy submerged in a wave of self-reproach.

'I'm sorry,' she said, bowing her head to his shoulder.

His smile was reflected in his voice, very tender, very loving. Though the hand he ran from her shoulder to her thigh as he moved her over to lie beside him was frankly predatory, the lazy touch of it deliberate and erotic.

'So am I,' he said blandly. 'She has a knack for picking her times. I'll have to go, my heart's dear delight.'

CHAPTER EIGHT

BACK in her own apartment Melly made herself a cup of coffee and reflected without bitterness that thanks to Cathy's phone call she felt like a girl-friend hurriedly hustled out of the way when the legitimate wife put in an appearance.

Totally irrational, of course. Today was clearly her day for illogical thinking—and feeling. A storm of colour embarrased her as she remembered just how it had been with them, her frenzied reaction to the near-violence of Trent's initial possession and the way her body had responded without restraint to the wild sweetness his had engendered in her.

Very blasé, trying hard for some sort of sophistication to hide the overwhelming impact his lovemaking had made on her, she told herself that few virgins could have had a better introduction to the world of sensual gratification.

Perhaps, if she covered it with pompous, ludicrous phrases culled from pop psychology, she might be able to conceal from herself the fact that he had shattered every one of the defences erected with so much difficulty over the years. The act of love had smashed down the civilised barriers she had set between her mind and her body, allowing him to invade and possess himself of both. Making love was not civilised, of course. It was a primitive earthy drive, as basic as the need to eat and to sleep, and the rosy veils that civilisation tried to impose on it were ripped away by the raw emotions which accompanied the act of love. Sex, she thought ironically, was not exactly romantic. Overwhelming, stupendous, a fierce knitting together of sensation and emotion until the only way to express them was that tumultuous climax when mind and heart and body were welded together in the union of two separate, unique people.

And yet, for all the almost frightening loss of control, there had been tenderness and a giving which now, when she recalled it, brought stupid tears to her eyes. In spite of his uninhibited hunger for the release her body could give him, Trent had used her with generosity and care and a loving thoughtfulness which made her heart ache.

Finally, now, after he had made himself master of her in that most primitive of ways, she was forced to admit that his desire for her was rooted in love.

The sun spilled golden across the smooth surface of a wide glass table in the sitting-room, dimpling the coffee in her cup with coins of gold. Melly's head was lowered, her eyes thoughtful and sober as she lifted the cup and drank. Once she had admitted her love for him this latest admission had been inevitable, she realised, but it still came as a shock. Not a very pleasant one.

While she was convinced that he had only wanted her, her emotions had been understandable and easily controlled. The strong physical attraction between them had been just that, the desire of the eye, the pull of virile male for innocent female. She could accept that and control it, her confidence unabated.

But now that she had to accept a far more sobering fact, she was deathly afraid. For if she loved him and he loved her they would marry. Her hungry heart would make it inevitable.

And she would love him with all the fervour of a woman long denied, love him—and spend her life wondering how much he could be trusted. Each new obstacle, each handicap in their life would be greater in impact because it might be the one to separate them. That marriage to Cathy had revealed that he was an opportunist willing to sacrifice anything to his hunger for ascendancy. Even if he never again had to choose between love and power, her knowledge of the flaw in his character would poison their life together.

He was so strong, she mused, unaware of the wistfulness in her expression. Strong and tender, yet the opportunism that had driven him into that marriage was part of him too.

'I don't care,' she whispered, rocking back and forwards in the warmth of the sun because it was the only way to ease the pain in her. 'I don't care—I love him.'

And her mind roved back to recall the ecstatic rightness of their lovemaking, the incredible perfection of the whole experience. A long time later she found herself hoping that she was pregnant, because that would take the decision out of her hands. She would be able to give in to pressure without feeling so overpowered!

Only for a few seconds, until the real Melly Hollingworth, the intelligent woman who was not weakened by a foolish passion for a flawed lover, came to the fore once again. How despicably weak, to hope for an Act of God to take the decision out of her hands.

Straightening shoulders which had slumped, she got to her feet, her features set, almost rigid. Until she had made that decision, she must keep him at a distance. There must be no more lovemaking to sap her willpower in a fog of sweet sensuality. It was vital to keep a clear brain to deal with the issues; it was, after all, her life she was deciding.

When the telephone rang she knew she had been waiting for it.

'Melissa?' said Trent, sounding tired. 'I'm afraid it looks as though I'll be here all day.'

'Lady Durrant?'

'She's had a bad asthma attack and somebody has to stay with Cathy.'

Although Melly's knuckles whitened on the receiver at the note of concern and affection she heard in his voice she had to admit that his solicitude for his ex-wife was strangely endearing. Tonelessly she responded, 'Yes, of course.'

'Darling, I didn't want this. I wish I was with you now.' He paused, then finished harshly, 'I can hear the cogs turning in that brain of yours! Just don't forget that I can make you so mindless that you can only beg me to pleasure you.'

In spite of her misery her body dissolved in a spasm of liquid fire. She must have made some sort of sound, because she heard his mirthless chuckle before, speaking quickly as though someone had come into the room, he said, 'Goodbye, dear heart. I'll see you tonight when I get home.'

'No!' But he'd already hung up, and she was left to put the receiver down while her whole body trembled with a sensuous yearning.

And when, just before she went to bed, the telephone rang again, she spoke harshly into it.

'I can't get back,' Trent said bluntly. 'I think she's dying.'

'Oh—Trent!' The shameful anger and rejection fled. 'I'm so sorry. Is there anything I can do?'

'No. Just remember that I love you.'

Lady Durrant's death made the morning newspaper. Saddened, Melly read it over breakfast. The old lady's son and only child had been killed two years after his daughter's birth, leaving Cathy as her only living descendant. Sir Peter's industrial empire was mentioned in passing with an allusion to Trent, but most of the paragraph was taken up with mention of Lady Durrant's favourite charities—all of them, Melly noted, to do with children.

And as she caught the bus to work Melly couldn't help wondering just how much comfort Cathy Durrant needed now.

It took her almost all the trip to banish the jealous little thought. However resolutely she pushed it away it returned like a nagging toothache, fretting away at the edge of her consciousness so that she welcomed the discipline her work imposed.

Unfortunately she could not evade it even there. Somehow, by that mysterious growth known as the grapevine, it had become known that Trent was with Cathy, and Susan Field was avid, irritating Melly so much with speculation that she refused an invitation to eat lunch with her on the pretext that she had shopping to do.

So she made a rather miserable pilgrimage to a big department store, wandering around aimlessly before buying a wooden Noah's Ark for Dougal's Christmas present and a frivolous scarf the exact colour of Jennet's green eyes. It was on her way back to work that she saw them, Trent, tall and austere in a sombre dark suit, with Cathy Durrant clinging to his arm as they came out from a suite of professional chambers to a waiting taxi.

Faltering, her whole being suddenly racked with wretchedness, Melly stared at them, her bitter possessive eyes noting the way Cathy's brilliant head rested on Trent's shoulder as though he was her only source of strength. Trent looked impossibly remote, his hard features set in lines that aged him. There was a kind of pity and a gentle solicitude in his attitude towards the bereft girl which made Melly bite hard down on her lip. Yet although the raw feeling of jealousy was predominant, another, more poignant emotion brought a suspicion of tears to her eyes. Wistfully she found herself wishing he could guard her with that protective attitude.

Stupid! But she could not rid herself of the desolation which had invaded her at the sight of them together. Not then, and not in the lonely days that followed.

Trent had not come home, she was sure, since the day he had seduced her, and he did not ring.

Just another example of how little she really meant to him. Not even to herself did she admit how much she needed reassurance and comfort. He had awakened the responses of her untried body and now she was prey to hungers she had never before experienced. At night she lay wakeful, staring into the darkness with hot eyes while resentment hardened in some vulnerable hidden part of her.

That weekend she went up to Te Puriri, taking a commercial flight on Friday night and returning early Monday morning with Rafe, who brought her back in the small plane he kept for just such occasions.

He dropped her off at work and went about his business with lawyers and accountants, the structure that kept all the Hollingworth interests manageable and profitable. He would be staying for several days.

'Why don't you come too, Jennet?' Melly asked hopefully.

Her half-sister exchanged a complicated look with Rafe. 'Because I'm pregnant,' she said cheerfully, 'and feeling slightly queasy. I'm better off here.'

So that had been a cause for rejoicing, yet the weekend, pleasant though it had been, had only exacerbated the raw, painful misery Melly was feeling.

Halfway down Rafe said calmly, 'What's the matter, love?' The fact that Rafe was so much older than her had been one of the reasons for Melly's childish hero-worship of him, but they had stronger ties than that, for in many ways he had been the only person she could trust. Yet the circumstances of their childhood had made for a quality of self-sufficiency in each. Much as she loved him, confident as she was of his love for her, she could no longer confide in him.

'I need my mummy,' she said ironically, her voice revealing too much for him to misunderstand.

As in many strong men, Rafe's protective instinct was particularly well developed, but although he frowned he did not try to coax her into revelations she might regret.

After one penetrating glance at her aloof profile all he said was, 'I can no longer promise to make things right for you, but I can promise you an ear—and no criticism.'

'I know.'

Melly was touched, her voice suddenly husky. 'I do love you, Rafe. If there was anything you could do, I'd ask, believe me. I have to fight my way through this by myself.'

And never had she felt so alone, so isolated without guidelines or a path. Still, having Rafe with her for those few days made a huge difference. He took her out to dinner at a very exclusive restaurant and made her heart swell with pride when she saw how women watched him. He and Trent both possessed a natural authority, inbuilt, dominant, which drew automatic recognition and appreciative, covert glances. In fact, she drew so much comfort from him that she began to understand why Cathy clung to Trent.

On the night before he flew back to Te Puriri he said, 'I've promised to go to a party at the Wetheralls'. I must have been mad. Do you want to come?'

'Oh no . . .' Melly stopped, then shrugged. 'Why not?' she said lightly. 'I've never been to one of their parties. Rather wild, aren't they?'

He grinned. 'Oh, as with all of us, the years have quietened them down. Would I take my young sister to a wild party?'

'Who better? I can have all of the fun of watching without being afraid that someone might run off with me!'

She did not know that his suggestion had softened the rigid, sleepwalker's countenance she had worn since the weekend. Beneath that stony, frightening self-control a spark of anticipation gave her some animation. Rafe saw it and was relieved.

'Put something outrageous on,' he commanded.

'What are you going to wear?'

One black brow lifted in self-mockery. 'Oh, I'm too old a married man for trendy clothes.'

But he looked very, very attractive in narrow dark trousers and an elegant silk shirt cut somewhat like a Cossack smock. Melly, who preferred timelessly elegant clothes, widened her eyes at him as she came into the sitting-room in a silk jersey sheath of deep, glowing crimson, one-shouldered with two large ruffles at knee-level.

'How do you think we look?' she asked, swirling for him.

'Oh, very ethnic.'

She grinned at the dry note in his voice and they left, well pleased with each other.

Fiona and Paul Wetherall were a couple whose basic insecurity was pointed up by their determined pursuit of the latest trends. That they did not make fools of themselves was due to a basic core of common sense and humour, with enough inclination to laugh at themselves to prevent the worst excesses such a way of life could give rise to.

Melly had heard of their parties; indeed, when she had left New Zealand they were spoken of in slightly scandalised tones, but as she gazed around the enormous basement room where this one was being held she couldn't help but feel that the reality was not nearly as interesting as the gossip.

There were all types and descriptions of people, from a large, very shaggy man clearly left over from the sixties to several young things in the latest fashions, their faces mask-like with superb make-up except for their alert, almost avid eyes.

Several people Melly recognised as television personalities, there was an English actor who was out in

New Zealand to make a series of extremely expensive commercials, and a small pale woman who had written an historical novel which had had blockbuster sales in America.

And there was Trent, his arm around Cathy Durrant's waist, her beautiful, pale face lifted to his in appealing melancholy.

After the first incredulous seconds Melly behaved very well. She smiled and talked and held a glass of white wine and was introduced to people, and she must have sounded normal, because no one looked sideways at her. Yet she couldn't remember a word she had said, or the name of a person she had met, and when she met Rafe's eyes she saw concern in them backed by a hard antagonism which meant that he knew why she was so tense.

It had to happen, of course, but when she heard Trent's voice behind her, her heart lunged in her breast and she could not move. Beside her Rafe turned his head; the two men must have stared each other down for long seconds, aggression crackling between them, until Melly found the strength to face Trent, her eyes hard and glazed, revealing nothing as they searched the lean, reckless features. He too was giving nothing away.

'Hello, Trent,' she said in a surprisingly steady voice.

He withdrew his gaze from Rafe's and smiled at her, that quick, feral grin which was his trademark. 'You look—superb. Come and dance with me.'

Vaguely she said, 'What about Cathy? Didn't you come——'

'Oh, she's with her boy-friend,' he said easily, the only indication that he was aware of Rafe's hostility the quick lifting of his head and the savage taunting quality to his glance.

Without further protest she accompanied him, trembling as his arm slid around her waist, as their bodies touched, pulled away, met again.

'Relax,' he murmured softly, bending his head to touch his lips to her temple. 'What have you been doing since last I saw you? Missing me?'

At that moment she hated him. Stormy eyes revealed her emotions, eyes black as obsidian, heated with the strength of her emotions. He smiled, revealing cynicism shot through with an odd sympathy.

'I would have rung, but it seemed better not to. I couldn't say what I wanted to over the phone.'

'And that was?'

Trent lowered his head, whispering, 'That I miss you and need you and hunger for you, day and night. That to hear your voice is a sweet torment, and the days I don't see you are bitter and everlasting.'

Emotion shivered through her in answer to the starkness of his words. It was agony to hold herself stiffly away from him; she winced, looking about to meet Cathy Durrant's wide blue eyes, the speculation in them not hiding a kind of astonished anger.

It was like being thrown into Polar seas. In a tight, hard voice she said, 'Your ex-wife is wondering what tales you're spinning. She doesn't look exactly pleased.'

'She's spoiled and possessive,' he said bluntly, 'but she knows she has no claim on me.'

'I thought you said she was shattered by her grandmother's death.'

He responded to the accusing note in her voice with a bland smile, those penetrating eyes too aware of the angry jealousy she was trying so hard to hide. 'Don't be fooled by that glossy exterior she presents. She's had to learn to hide her feelings. It took both her boy-friend's and my persuasions to coax her out tonight; she thought it would be disrespectful.'

He turned his head, watching the girl as she listened to their host. Melly would have given everything she possessed to know exactly what thoughts lay behind the mask of his features. When he turned back to look down into her face her lips parted, trembling.

Abruptly he finished, 'She's not exactly enjoying herself, Melly.'

'Neither am I,' she said beneath her breath. 'Nor you, Trent. This is no good, can't you see that?'

'No.' All the will she recognised in the man was contained in that monosyllable, an inflexible purposefulness that made her tremble with a sense of her own weakness.

He pulled her closer, holding her in an embrace which had little of passion, much tenderness in it. Yet there was no easing of that dreadful determination when he spoke. 'My sweet lady, I know why you're fighting me, I understand how you feel, but I'm not going to let your scruples and that fear you've always felt ruin the only good thing in my life.'

'How *can* you say that?' Her disbelief was written in the face she lifted to him. 'If I asked you to give up everything for me, to abandon your work, would you do that?'

She felt tension harden his body, sharpen his features so that for a moment he looked like an eagle swooping on its prey. 'Is that what you want me to do?' he asked with a quiet lack of emphasis.

Wearily she shook her head. 'Of course not. I have no right to ask such a sacrifice of you. Apart from anything else, so many people depend on you for their livelihood. And you enjoy your work, don't you, Trent?'

'It's been the only thing that kept me sane these last years,' he conceded curtly. 'But even if I'd hated it, I couldn't have agreed to give it up. I promised Sir Peter.' He smiled sardonically, meeting her troubled eyes with a complete lack of humour. 'I can justify myself by quoting poetry, you know. Isn't poetry supposed to be a high truth? *"I could not love thee, dear, so much, loved I not honour more,"* I'm afraid it applies.'

Melly shook her head, exhausted. 'I told you, I wouldn't ask that of you. You'd wither and die without the cut and thrust of your life. Do you think I haven't heard the stories?' Her smile trembled, faded. 'I'm not exactly segregated, even if I do lurk in the library. Your staff like nothing better than to regale each other with stories of your prowess, your brilliant brain, your ruthless buccaneering in your chosen field. I have no right to ask you to give it up.'

'You know me so well.' It was not exactly a compliment, but before the taunt behind it had time to register he continued, 'We know each other so well, you and I, we always have after that first long look. Melissa, can't you let your mind overtake your heart? All that you need do is trust me when I say that I wouldn't hurt you now, that last time it was like cutting my heart out. I did it because you were overseas; I couldn't have told you to your face.' Thickly he finished, 'If you'd been here, I wouldn't have needed to.'

Melly bit her lip, torn by anguish and the corroding bitterness she could not rid herself of. 'I'm sorry,' she said, wondering even as the words left her lips why she was apologising.

'You look—exhausted.' Trent's voice was grim, without expression. 'You should be home, sleeping. How long is big brother staying?'

Startled, for she had forgotten Rafe's presence, she looked around the enormous room until she saw him, leaning against the wall as he spoke to an elderly man with a sharp, predatory face.

'He's going back tomorrow,' she said in a stifled voice. 'Trent—I don't want to see you again. Please, don't make a nuisance of yourself or—or I'll have to leave Auckland.'

The muscles beneath her hand tensed, then relaxed. 'Very well,' he said aloofly, adding with a twisted smile, 'I don't want to hurt you, darling, and that's what I've been doing, isn't it?'

Her heart ached, for if he had hurt her she knew now that she was hurting him too, and that knowledge was bitter grief.

'It won't work out,' she said, confused, her voice arid. 'It—we've been doomed right from the start. Oh God, I'm chattering away in clichés. Where's Rafe?'

'I'll take you to him.'

Half an hour later Melly was huddled in her bed, trying to smother the sounds of her weeping in her pillow. She didn't hear the door open, or see the bar of light across the floor eclipsed by Rafe's tall outline; the first she knew of his presence was his hand on her shoulder and the muttered curse he gave when her sobs died down sufficiently for her to hear anything at all.

After a while he asked calmly, 'Don't you think you'd better tell me? Getting it off your chest might ease things.'

So she told him everything, her voice gradually picking up strength as she regained control, until at last it faded away into silence.

'I see,' Rafe said evenly, and for a long time there was silence in the dimly-lit room. Then he said, 'Have you ever thought that you might be wrong, Melly?'

The slender hand in his twisted. 'I've often wished it, but what other reason could there have been?'

'Oh, I can think of several.' Rafe got up from his seat on the side of the bed and walked across to the window. 'Several,' he said again, thoughtfully.

'Such as?'

'Blackmail. Old Peter Durrant was a hard man. The only chink in his armour was Cathy. He may have wanted to secure her future and decided that Addison was the way to do it.'

Melly gasped, then sighed. 'Can you honestly see Trent knuckling under to blackmail?' she asked.

Rafe's head turned and there was a flash of white as he smiled. 'No, my dear, but I can't imagine him

marrying the girl just to get his hands on Durrant
Holdings, either. Don't forget I went to school with
him. A man's basic character doesn't change that much.
He was ambitious but honourable. And don't forget
that Sir Peter had an immense amount of power. If I
remember rightly Trent had stretched himself to the
limit at that time, getting his firm off the ground. It
wouldn't have been difficult for the old man to have put
pressure on him in some way. You know as well as I do
that such things happen.'

One part of Melly wanted to believe him, to grasp at
his solution so much that she thought she could taste
the wanting in her mouth.

Long fingers plucked at the sheet as she said tiredly,
'Then why won't he tell me? He's refused to give me
any reason for what happened.'

'Perhaps,' Rafe suggested, 'he wants you to trust him.'

'How can I?' It was the wail of a child, infantile yet
all the more compelling for that.

'I don't know. All in all, he had every right to think
you're swayed by passion when you're with him, but
that your mind is coldly aware of his deficiencies. No
man wants to be loved in spite of his faults, Melly. It's
too much to demand that we be loved for them, but
they must be accepted. Have you ever thought that you
require that he prove himself perfect before you'll
marry him?'

'No!' She sat upright in the bed, indignation
trembling in her voice.

But Rafe was merciless. 'Yes. I think perhaps it's a
Hollingworth characteristic. We insist on impossibly
high standards before we can trust. I almost lost Jennet
because I wouldn't trust her. And if I had lost her,
Melly, my life would have been as empty and as
wearisome to me as imprisonment in the pits of hell.'
He paused, then went on, 'Ask yourself what your life
would be like without Addison.'

'I managed before,' she said in a muted voice. 'I was happy enough.'

'Were you?'

Her eyes lowered to the sheet across her knees. Almost sullenly she said, 'No.'

'Why did you come back?'

She could have lied, but the habit of telling Rafe the truth was too deeply ingrained. 'Because Jennet wrote to me that Trent's divorce was final. And that's the first time that I've ever admitted that, even to myself.'

Rafe came back and kissed her cheek. 'Then don't you think you'd better admit a few more things? Like the fact that you're hopelessly in love with the man?'

'I don't want to be.'

'I know the feeling,' he told her drily as he straightened. 'You don't want the pain and the turmoil and the naked defencelessness—oh, I know. You want to remain fully in control, where nothing can touch you. But that's the coward's way, Melly, and you're not a coward.'

He left her with that and she lay back into the pillows, wondering. Trust Rafe to be so blunt, she thought, and then, indignantly, but it's not cowardly to try to protect yourself, surely?

Eventually she slept and woke next morning still refusing to accept her brother's assessment of the situation. She did not admit that she dared not; she told herself sturdily that she had every right to be suspicious of the man who had let her down so badly before.

And she drove her car off to work determined that from now on she was going to make it quite obvious to Trent that there was no future for them. It was as if she had grown an impervious skin over her heart. So it was all the more bewildering after several days to realise that Trent must have come to the same conclusion, and she was appalled at the depths of her despair.

By the weekend she had forced herself to accept that

he wasn't going to make any effort to contact her. She knew he was back in his apartment; sometimes she saw the car in the car park, quite often when she came up the drive after running her frustration off, her eyes noted a light from the rooms in the penthouse.

On Friday night she went out with a group from the social club to the speedway and endured an evening of loud engine noise and an almost total lack of interest, which was infuriating, because normally she would have enjoyed it. Trent was out, too; his car was gone. It didn't reappear all weekend and she endured a kind of agonised disquiet wondering if it was Cathy who kept him away.

Slowly during the following weeks she began to realise that Auckland was just as lonely as London had been. Swiftly the year surged on towards Christmas; she bought presents, made plans for the holidays and found her evenings being filled by parties and dinners as more and more of her friends realised that she was home. She went everywhere, keeping thought at bay, and only Sara Horning noticed the gradual sharpening of her features which was the only outward sign of an intolerable self-restraint.

Sara, and Susan Field at work, who said with characteristic bluntness, 'By the look of you you've been burning the candle at both ends. Why don't you get a good night's sleep for a change?'

Why not indeed? Melly returned some conventional answer because she couldn't tell Susan the truth, that what time was left to her for sleep was an endless purgatory of longing. Better by far to go out where there was something to occupy her mind, even if it was only dinner party chatter and the kind of gossip she found boring and empty.

Sara was incredibly tactful, but she had just discovered that she was pregnant and Melly couldn't dim her delight by telling her how bitterly, drearily

miserable she was. Not that she was a great one for
confidences, anyway. Rafe and Jennet were the only
people she could have unburdened herself to and they
were a hundred and fifty miles away.

So she plodded on stoically, telling herself that it had
been like this before and she had got over that; this too
would pass. But before she had had only memories of
the restrained gentleness of Trent's embraces while now
she lay sweating in her bed as she remembered how it
had been with them when he had made himself master
of her body.

She had no defences against memory. Until that day
she had been physically unawakened, unaware of what
desire could do. Now she knew, and ached for his
touch, the ecstasy he had wrung from her with his
possession. When she closed her eyes she could see the
long, lean lines of his body, the whipcord strength
which had overpowered her before the sensual magic of
his lovemaking had brought about her complete
submission.

She knew hunger, discovered the tyranny of desire,
wept because she could not close her eyes without those
disturbing images dancing on her eyelids; the two of
them lying on his huge bed, intertwined, gold skin
against olive, the way his hand stroked her from armpit
to hip as if he loved the sensations fed to him by
fingertip and palm . . .

Oh, she knew despair, and anger, and a deeper, more
basic emotion than those, the anguish of being only a half,
with the complementing other part of her torn free.

But she fought it, afraid of her dependence on him,
stubbornly refusing to accept that she needed him in
every way besides the physical. In her own way she
betrayed herself, calling what she felt the ugliest name
she could find. Lust, she whispered into the darkness,
because she was too afraid to accept that her desire was
irradiated by love.

CHAPTER NINE

'YOU'LL have to come,' Sara pleaded. 'It's terribly important to Jim that the firm get this account. Just think of it, legal retainer to such an enormous conglomerate!'

'It's a wonderful opportunity,' Melly replied a little vaguely, as she tended to be nowadays.

Sara nodded, stirring her coffee guiltily. 'I shouldn't take sugar, I know, but I can't face tea and I can't cope with coffee black and I daren't use an artificial sweetener. The baby,' she explained at her companion's blank look of enquiry.

'Oh, yes, although I didn't think——'

'My doctor is exceptionally fussy, but I agree with him. So you will come, Mel?'

'Of course I'll come.' Melly couldn't refuse, and didn't really want to. When Sara had rung her up and suggested meeting for lunch in town she had detected a strained note in her friend's voice. Now, with all explained, she understood. Apart from one thing.

'Why you?' she asked. 'I mean, I'd have thought that Jim's parents would have entertained this tycoon.'

'Mrs Horning isn't well. She's got high blood pressure and they're having difficulty in stabilising it. She won't even be able to come, which is why I want you there, Mel, to give me moral support. You're marvellous at a dinner party, you know how to keep people amused . . .'

'Now don't go getting yourself worked up into a tizz,' Melly recommended cheerfully. 'So are you, and you know it. You're also a wonderful cook. What are you going to feed the brute on?'

'Something simple and superb,' Sara told her, her expressive face thoughtful. 'Dane Fowler lives in Fiji, but he's cosmopolitan. He has interests all around the Pacific, shipping, plantations, mines—you name it, they've got it. He'll have eaten the best the world can offer, so I'm not even going to try to compete. We have magnificent meat and fruit and vegetables. I'll let them speak for themselves.'

'Good. You can do it, none better. Who else will be there?'

'Well . . .' Sara looked self-conscious suddenly. 'Mrs Fowler and an associate of theirs. Thea Graham, will be his partner. Jim's father and his aunt Marie, and—oh, hell, I've asked Trent and he's coming too!'

For a moment the rapidly rattled out words didn't register. When they did Melly felt the colour drain from her skin and her hands clenched in her lap. She looked across the table, to meet Sara's imploring gaze.

'I see,' she said tonelessly. Then, without even thinking, because she had some pride, 'Well, it will be the first time I've seen him for quite a while.'

'Want to talk about it?' asked Sara sympathetically.

Melly shook her head. 'No, there's nothing to talk about. What time do you want me to come?'

'As early as you get there.'

An idea made Melly suggest, 'How would it be if I came after work? I could help you with any last-minute arrangements.'

'Oh, that would be lovely! And stay the night. That way we could talk things over afterwards, which is always the best part, I think, only Jim invariably wants to go to bed!'

That way Melly had a perfectly good excuse for not going with Trent. If he asked her.

He rang that evening and when she told him what her plans were said calmly and politely, 'Right then, I'll look forward to seeing you there.'

That was when she gave up hope.

Auckland looked its best as she drove to the Hornings'. The leafy suburb they lived in was one of the prettiest in the city. Not even the rush-hour traffic, she thought grimly as she avoided a little white MG apparently bent on suicide, could prevent her from enjoying the drive. As she turned beneath a great pohutukawa tree crimson with its strange, brushlike flowers, she concentrated fiercely on Sara's garden, gracious now with elegant orchid-like bearded irises in almost all shades except true red. A little further along silken Californian poppies held their skirts of pink and orange aloft, contrasting with silver-blue stars of campanula against their vivid almond foliage.

It was a delicious afternoon, drowsily hot, yet the influence of the little volcano with its grassy slopes lent a pastoral freshness to the air.

Sara, however, looked far from fresh. 'Oh, I'm in such a muddle!' she wailed, pushing back a lock of hair with a grubby hand. 'Everything that could go wrong has, and I know I'm not going to be able to do it!'

'Yes, you can,' Melly told her lovingly. 'Now what's to be done?'

Her calm good sense was soothing and the extra pair of hands wrought such a difference that by the time Jim arrived home his house was ready, the dinner was as advanced as it should be and his wife had recovered her nerve.

She lost it again five minutes before the guests were due to arrive, running her hands down the front of her pretty embroidered cotton dress to ask anxiously, 'Are you *sure* you can't see that I'm pregnant?'

'Quite sure,' Melly and Jim answered for the third time. Jim gave his wife a hug, adding with a leer, 'You look delectable enough to eat, darling.'

'I just hope the dinner does,' Sara said gloomily.

The Fowlers were a stunning couple, he tall and dark

and good-looking in a rather fierce way, she with a bell
of blonde hair about a pointed, triangular face and a
sweet, rather mischievous smile. They arrived a few
minutes after the others, but before Trent, who drove
up just as Sara was beginning to look anxious. He
apologised with his usual suavity, charming Sara into
smiles instantaneously.

He looked tired, Melly thought, casting him a swift
little glance from beneath her lashes. But when he
smiled the shadow lifted from his face and she decided
she had been wrong.

He knew the Fowlers; later she was to find that he
had helped Dane Fowler to computerise his whole
operation. For the moment she watched, quietly sipping
white wine, while he talked with Jim's father, a hand in
his trouser pocket, his stance relaxed yet vigilant. Like a
wild animal, she thought, with an animal's lean, sinewy
grace and its constant alertness.

And every cell in her body clamoured for him in a
wave of sensation so intense that she could do nothing
but wait, stricken, for it to ebb away. The glass in her
hand shook, making little catspaws across the pale
wine. She looked up and he was watching her, and in
his hard eyes there was nothing, no emotion, no
recognition. It was as though she was totally invisible.

Stung, her pride reared and she smiled at him,
deliberately. He smiled back, but it didn't reach those
cold eyes; all she could read there was an icy mockery
until Mr Horning said something and Trent turned
politely back to him.

It was like being slapped in the face. For a moment
Melly was furious, but she folded her lips in a way her
sister would have recognised and set herself out to be a
charming and perfect guest.

Although this was business masquerading as a
private party, a sort of job interview in disguise, it soon
became a very friendly interview. The Fowlers were fun,

witty, intelligent and not in the least patronising in spite of their wealth and influence. Sara lost most of her nervousness, a process helped by Meredith Fowler's involuntary exclamation of pleasure when she saw the dinner-table for the first time.

'You have an artist's eye,' she said admiringly. 'It looks beautiful, Sara.'

Sara showed her appreciation with a blush, but Mrs Fowler had been right. The table was beautifully set with simple modern silver and white porcelain plates. Beneath them was a cloth of dark crimson. For the flowers Sara had chosen cottage pinks in shades of rose and crimson and red; the scent floated evocatively above the table while their colours blended with the seafood cocktail Sara had set out, a tropical fantasy with pawpaw and avocado providing a perfect background to striped shrimp and slices of smoked salmon.

After that, no one could doubt that Sara's dinner party was a success. All anxiety forgotten, she relaxed and became her usual pert self, while Jim beamed with pride.

Dane Fowler's associate turned out to be a very smooth man of about thirty-five or so, good-looking in a bland conventional way, with a pleasant manner which didn't hide the fact that nothing escaped his opaque, shrewd eyes. His partner, Thea Graham, was recovering from a divorce, and by the way she was acting, Melly decided sourly, she was intent on celebrating her freedom.

Not that she was blatant. She was not above using her very considerable physical attributes to gain attention, and if it had been her partner she was displaying them for Melly would have wished her good luck with a smile.

But Thea, after exchanging pleasantries with John Goudge, moved on to more important game, and was using every bit of her wit and style, not to mention those stunning physical assets, to attract Trent. And he, the swine, was clearly not in the least averse to voluptuous blondes with ambiguous smiles and quick provocative repartee. He was not obvious, either, his excellent bone-deep manners saw to that. Both he and Thea kept the conversational ball going, but they smiled rather too frequently at each other and there was that invisible aura about them that proclaimed their interest in each other as clearly as if they had shouted it to the stars.

Melly was furious, her anger rooted in a desolation so intense that it ached in her bones. She could not bear to watch their elegant flirtation, so she turned to John Goudge, deliberately coasting by on the social graces her mother had drilled into her.

By the time dinner came to an end she wanted nothing more than to burst into tears and retire to bed to nurse a heart she had finally to admit was broken. The fact that it was all her own doing made her so frustrated that she could have screamed.

Unfortunately for Melly, for everyone else the evening continued so enjoyably that it dragged on and on, no one wanting to break it up. Melly saw Trent smiling with practised sophistication into Thea's face and had to fight the impulse to fling her coffee over him and declare trenchantly that he belonged to her. This fierce sense of possession appalled her; she had never before realised how jealousy could scale the soul even when, like hers, it was founded on a sense of betrayal which was unbearable.

Once more she set her jaw and turned to John Goudge, who seemed unaware of the undercurrents that seethed around him, as did everyone else. Somehow she managed to get through the evening, even to join in Sara's happy recapitulation of everything until it was so late that she fell asleep the moment her body slid gratefully between the sheets. But the next morning she woke up knowing that she was going to have to leave Auckland. She just could not take Trent's wooing of another woman, whoever she was, and she was far too likely to meet him both socially and at work.

Over a late breakfast Sara chattered cheerfully, once more discussing the Fowlers and the evening while Jim and Melly drank coffee in companionable silence.

'Meredith Fowler has a little boy,' Sara said, 'almost two, she told me, but she also has a young brother of five. She was awfully nice, wasn't she?'

Melly nodded, Jim grunted. Not at all put off by such a reception, she went on, 'And he is gorgeous, isn't he? Dane Fowler, I mean. Did you notice his eyes? A funny sort of yellowy-brown. He reminded me of Trent, a bit.'

Another grunt from Jim, but this time Melly lifted lacklustre eyes enquiringly. 'Dane Fowler has to be one of the best-looking men I've seen,' she said. 'No one could call Trent handsome.'

'He doesn't need to be, does he? John Goudge has more regular classically handsome features, but Thea made no play for him! She took one look at Trent and knew instantly that he offered far more than John. No,' Sara repeated somewhat insensitively, Melly felt, 'Dane and Trent have that masculine authority that's so immensely attractive to women.'

Jim swallowed half a cup of coffee before demanding plaintively, 'Yeah, but what exactly is it? They're both rich—is that what turns you on?'

'If it was, would I have married you?' Sara exchanged a complicated glance with Melly before trying to explain the unexplainable. 'Trent has it. So does Dane and Mel's brother, Rafe, for that matter. But we know Trent best, so let's use him as an example. He's—well, he's strong. I don't mean physically, though that probably helps, but he has this air of competence, as though there's nothing he couldn't cope with. For example, you can't imagine him having a tantrum because the car won't start. And it's not that he would know exactly what to do to make the thing go, he may know nothing about engines, but you only have to look at him to realise that he'd get it fixed somehow. He has authority.' Her brow wrinkled as she sought for words. 'And you feel that he values women, that if he were your lover you'd be—*important* to him. As well as pleasured to within an inch of your life,' she finished, her small face alight with wicked humour.

Melly felt her cheeks heat under the impact of memories she was trying to repress. Hastily she dragged her attention back to Jim, who was saying, 'But I thought women were supposed to be competent themselves nowadays. If so, how can you find a man's self-confidence sexy?'

'It's not just that is it, Mel? And authority is a better word than confidence. It's the combination of strength and dominance and the capacity to be gentle and tender, as well as the knowledge that he's a superb lover.'

'And how do you know that?' Jim asked sceptically.

Sara's eyes danced. 'Darling, we may think we're rational beings, but instincts play a large part in our lives. I'll bet you can tell at a glance whether you'd like to go to bed with a woman, and I'll bet your brain doesn't have much to do with the decision.'

'I have,' Jim told her with dignity, 'given that sort of thing up since I got married.'

'Not even a stray, hastily hidden, wistful little recognition?'

He grinned. 'No,' he said firmly. 'Well, not often, anyway.' And put up his hand to catch the croissant Sara threw at him. They smiled at each other with mutual appreciation, bringing something hot and envious to Melly's expression. Only for an instant. She liked them both so much and it was petty and self-

pitying to give way to envy of what they shared.
Natural, though, when she thought of how little she had
shared with Trent.

She left mid-morning, driving slowly back to The
Towers through a day warm and filled with the promise
of a New Zealand summer. Once the car was parked
she felt so disinclined to go up to the apartment that she
walked out of the building and down the drive beneath
the big old trees, unaware that her face was set in an
expression of desolation. For once the glowing gardens
failed to lift her spirits; she stood almost hesitantly
staring down into the crêpy white flowers of a rock-rose
as it sprawled on to the drive, watching as a praying
mantis slowly and stiffly stalked across the golden
throat, its evil triangular little face lifted sanctimoni-
ously above the cruel spiked forearms.

Death and beauty, Melly thought, shivering, as the
hum of a fly stilled the mantis instantly. Perhaps a
philosopher would ponder on the connection, but all
that she could think of now was the lazy anticipation in
Trent's eyes as he and Thea had left last night, and
although her stomach cramped she was no longer able
to stop herself from picturing them together, Trent's
hard body aroused and predatory, Thea all melting
response and seduction.

Quick, painful tears ached in her eyes. She blinked
fiercely, trying to banish from her too-faithful brain
that moment of agonised rapture when she had opened
her eyes and seen Trent's face carved in the involuntary
rictus of ecstasy. Heat flooded her body; she winced at
the urgent onset of feeling between her thighs and
turned blindly to walk across the road.

There was a blare of a horn and the squeal of brakes;
she had a fleeting vision of a mass of tumbled red and the
open mouth of a woman in the passenger's seat even as
her body obeyed reflex command older than time and
carried her out of danger to stand trembling in the sun

while Trent brought his car to a halt down the drive.

Numbly she waited while he got out of the car, slamming the door behind him as he walked, stiff-legged, back towards her. In the sun his hair gleamed almost as redly as that of Cathy Durrant, who had twisted around and was watching.

'You stupid little *bitch*!' he ground out, his face working as his hands shot out and fastened on to her shoulders.

Melly submitted to the fierce shaking he gave her without protest. Like her, he was high on adrenalin and it had to be dissipated somehow.

'Are you all right?' he demanded thickly, holding her away so that he could scan her face. 'Dear God, I thought——' He broke off and hauled her into his arms, holding her clamped so tightly against him that she could feel the tension in every muscle in his lean body. His chin crushed her unruly hair, flattening the curls against her skull. She could hear the tumbling race of his heart slow down, settle into the steady rhythm she knew, slow and regular, strong against her cheek. She could have stayed like this all day.

But he put her away from him and when her dazed eyes lifted he was the man she had seen last night, cool, worldly, his arrogance gleaming through the clear pale intimidating gaze.

'Next time,' he said gently, 'remember to look before you start to cross the road.'

The abrupt about-face disconcerted her into passing her tongue across her lips. Shakily she said, 'I'm sorry. I—the sun was too bright.'

'Then invest in a pair of sunglasses.' He smiled, not kindly. 'And take off the blinkers, Melissa, before they deprive you of everything you value.'

He wasn't talking about the incident just past. Her only defence was retaliation; she took a deep breath and tried hard for his brand of enigmatic sophistication.

'Oh, I never wear blinkers. Perhaps that's my trouble. I see too clearly.'

'Those who love their blindness . . .' Irony hardened his already hard smile. With insolent ease he used his forefinger to tip her chin, that remorseless gaze lingering on the pallor he found there, the strong lines of cheek and jaw and brow, the soft bow of her mouth.

'And you do, don't you,' he continued. 'You hug your blindness, your prejudices to you with a fervour worthy of a better cause.' His eyes dropped to her mouth for a significant second, moved to the high full curve of her breasts beneath the thin cotton shirt she wore over a denim skirt.

Frozen, Melly waited while his taunting scrutiny skimmed the feminine areas of her body, narrow waist, the bowl of her hips and the long lines of her thighs, pressed rigidly together to deny the source of the hot desire they protected. The dark lines of his face were almost scornful, yet with the acumen of a woman in love she realised that he wanted her, and for a moment she was gloatingly, bitterly satisfied with the fact.

Then reaction set in, twisting her mouth into a parody of a smile. 'I can guess what for,' she said bitterly as she stepped back.

The solid 'thunk' of a door closing did not break through their absorption in one another. It wasn't until Cathy Durrant's voice made both heads turn towards her that they remembered she was there.

'Trent, we really do have to go,' she said, her expression schooled into a blankness which did not extend to her eyes. 'Hello, Melly.'

'Cathy.' It was all she could say, and with no sign of a smile, either.

The younger woman hid her curiosity well. 'Sorry, but Trent and I have an appointment. We're going to be late,' she added when Trent said nothing.

He nodded, keeping his head averted so that Melly

1. How do you rate _____
   (Please print book TITLE)

   1.6 ☐ excellent   .4 ☐ good   .2 ☐ not so good
   .5 ☐ very good   .3 ☐ fair   .1 ☐ poor

BABCD

2. How likely are you to purchase another book:

   in this *series* ?   by this *author* ?

   2.1 ☐ definitely would purchase   3.1 ☐ definitely would purchase
   .2 ☐ probably would puchase   .2 ☐ probably would puchase
   .3 ☐ probably would not purchase   .3 ☐ probably would not purchase
   .4 ☐ definitely would not purchase   .4 ☐ definitely would not purchase

3. How does this book compare with similar books you usually read?

   4.1 ☐ far better than others   .2 ☐ better than others   .3 ☐ about the
   .4 ☐ not as good   .5 ☐ definitely not as good   same

4. Please check the statements you feel best describe this book.

   5. ☐ Easy to read   6. ☐ Too much violence/anger
   7. ☐ Realistic conflict   8. ☐ Wholesome/not too sexy
   9. ☐ Too sexy   10. ☐ Interesting characters
   11. ☐ Original plot   12. ☐ Especially romantic
   13. ☐ Not enough humor   14. ☐ Difficult to read
   15. ☐ Didn't like the subject   16. ☐ Good humor in story
   17. ☐ Too predictable   18. ☐ Not enough description of setting
   19. ☐ Believable characters   20. ☐ Fast paced
   21. ☐ Couldn't put the book down   22. ☐ Heroine too juvenile/weak/silly
   23. ☐ Made me feel good   24. ☐ Too many foreign/unfamiliar words
   25. ☐ Hero too dominating   26. ☐ Too wholesome/not sexy enough
   27. ☐ Not enough romance   28. ☐ Liked the setting
   29. ☐ Ideal hero   30. ☐ Heroine too independent
   31. ☐ Slow moving   32. ☐ Unrealistic conflict
   33. ☐ Not enough suspense   34. ☐ Sensuous/not too sexy
   35. ☐ Liked the subject   36. ☐ Too much description of setting

5. What *most* prompted you to buy this book?

   37. ☐ Read others in series   38. ☐ Title   39. ☐ Cover art
   40. ☐ Friend's recommendation   41. ☐ Author   42. ☐ In-store display
   43. ☐ TV, radio or magazine ad   44. ☐ Price   45. ☐ Story outline
   46. ☐ Ad inside other books   47. ☐ Other _____ (please specify)

6. Please indicate how many romance paperbacks you read in a month.

   48.1 ☐ 1 to 4   .2 ☐ 5 to 10   .3 ☐ 11 to 15   .4 ☐ more than 15

7. Please indicate your sex and age group.

   49.1 ☐ Male   50.1 ☐ under 15   .3 ☐ 25-34   .5 ☐ 50-64
   .2 ☐ Female   .2 ☐ 15-24   .4 ☐ 35-49   .6 ☐ 65 or older

8. Have you any additional comments about this book?

   _____ (51)
   _____ (53)

Thank you for completing and returning this questionnaire.

PRINTED IN U.S.A.

could see only the harsh, cutting line of his profile. 'I'm on my way.'

It was a dismissal, abrupt and discourteous. Cathy began to bridle, her chin coming up, but one glance from beneath her lashes at his unyielding countenance soon brought an end to that.

'Yes, well, I'll—nice to see you again, Melly,' she said, hiding her nervousness well. 'We must get together some time. I'm thinking of going to England soon; you must tell me where to go and what to do.'

'I'd like that,' Melly said huskily, lying, and knowing that Cathy had no intention of asking her.

Trent watched the erect, departing figure of his ex-wife with a narrowed intensity that tightened the hairs on the back of Melly's neck. When she was back in the car he swung his head to Melly again and said remotely, 'I'll be back in a couple of hours. We have to talk . . .'

'We've done enough of that.' She hesitated, then finished boldly, 'I don't want to see you, Trent. Why not look up Thea Graham? She isn't at all averse to your company, whereas I——'

'Whereas you hate my guts.' He spoke with sombre precision, permitting himself a slight shrug of those broad shoulders when her lashes lifted. His tanned skin seemed stretched over the incisive framework of his face; her fingers tingled as she remembered how he felt to her hands, the severe strength of bone and muscle allied to the sheer tactile pleasure of skin like warm silk and the forceful masculine symmetry of his body.

'Yes,' she said defiantly.

He smiled mirthlessly. 'I can always tell when you're lying. There are smudges beneath those polished eyes. Were you jealous of Thea Graham last night?'

'Did you want me to be?'

'Of course I did,' he said carelessly. 'Why should I be the only one to suffer? Don't try to run away from me, my heart. If I have to, I'll track you down to the limits of hell, but I won't be in the best mood when I find you.'

Melly watched as he strode off to the car, wishing forlornly that he wasn't able to turn her brain into mush with that cynical smile and the accident of birth that allowed him to move with the graceful power of a beast of prey.

Yet although she tried to convince herself that what she wanted from him was purely sexual she admitted, as she returned Cathy's wave of farewell, that really she wanted much, much more. His heart, his love, his respect.

All of him, for all of his life. Swiftly, before the car moved away, she turned back towards The Towers.

And although she stayed in all afternoon nobody rang for entry. Nobody—why nobody?—Trent did not come to her to tell her once more that he loved her, or to take from her the ease and pleasure he had found in her body.

When the telephone rang she jumped and went pale, her fingers trembling as she picked it up.

'Melly?'

Disappointment tightened her throat. 'Yes, Cathy.'

'Is Trent with you?'

She bit back on her anger, subduing it so that her voice was without expression. 'No, he's not. It is after nine, you know.'

'Yes, I know.' A pause. 'I want to see you. Will it be all right if I come in half an hour?'

'Now? Tonight?'

Cathy laughed, a cracked little sound with no humour at all in it. Yes. I'm afraid it's important.'

'Very well, then.'

Now why on earth had she agreed? The last person she ever wanted to see was Cathy Durrant!

And what did Cathy Durrant have to say to her that needed to be said at ten o'clock at night?

No answer came to her, except a pessimistic conviction that it was bound to be unpleasant. When the doorbell sounded it took all her willpower to open it to a rather defiant Cathy with sharp blue eyes and only a slight nervousness in her movements to reveal that beneath the glossy façade she wasn't nearly as self-assured as she seemed to be.

And in spite of Melly's efforts with make-up Cathy said after one all-encompassing look, 'You've been crying!'

It sounded like an accusation. Hastily Melly returned, 'A headache. I get them sometimes,' as she tried to hide her edginess.

'Doesn't everyone?' Cathy agreed gloomily before remembering her manners. 'Look, I know I'm—at least, there's something I have to tell you, and if you don't invite me in immediately and lock the door behind me I'll probably flee, and believe me, I'll never come back again, and that would be a pity.'

She wasn't just tense; she was terrified. The words had surged out in an agitated flood which left Melly even more bewildered, but she replied, 'I'm sorry, come on in. Can I make you a cup of coffee?'

'No,' Cathy said quietly. 'I think I'd better just sit down and tell all. You're not going to like it, but will you please remember that—all this happened when I was a very spoiled and idiotic eighteen-year-old?'

'Yes, of course.' By now Melly's nerves were stripped and exposed. She thought she knew what was coming and she did not want to listen. Mentally, physically and emotionally exhausted, she felt as though she had spent the last weeks fighting for her life. Now, when she needed her strength most, she was being worn down by Trent's unremitting pressure. Cathy's arrival was almost like the last straw.

'Just one thing,' Cathy said, seating herself in an armchair, 'do you mind very much reining in the exclamations? I don't need anyone to tell me how badly I've behaved. Believe me, no one could feel worse about it than I do. I've behaved like a—well, you'll see.'

Melly nodded, unable to make any sensible reply. As she too sat down, an uneasy little silence fell. Cathy was in no hurry to begin; she straightened the skirt of her pretty yellow dress, arranging her knees and legs and feet as carefully as if she was being photographed.

And then, when Melly thought she'd scream if the girl didn't begin soon, she transfixed Melly with those enormous eyes and asked in a gruff little voice, 'Are you in love with Trent?'

Melly's mouth fell open. 'What?' she said faintly.

'I can see you are.' Cathy shifted uneasily. 'I know he's in love with you now, but I've only just realised that he was in love with you when we married.'

'Then why did he marry you?'

'Because I—and my grandfather—forced him to.' Cathy folded her hands in her lap and leaned back against the chair, closing her eyes. 'I thought I was in love with him,' she went on in a hard little voice. 'I had the most almighty crush on him and I made a damned nuisance of myself. He was very kind about it. Then one night I told him I loved him and he was even kinder, he said that I'd find someone nearer my age—he was—oh, gentle and sweet, and I thought he was laughing at me.'

Her eyes snapped open again and she stared at Melly. 'He probably was. It must have been funny. I mean, there was I, eighteen and as innocent as—as a kitten— pouring out these protestations of undying love and passion, asking him to marry me . . .'

'I don't suppose Trent found it in the least amusing,' Melly said gently.

'Well, perhaps not, but I was totally humiliated. He let me down as lightly as possible, but believe it or not, that was the first setback I'd ever had. Up until then everything had gone my way. My mother let me do what I liked, I was as good as I wanted to be at school—I'm quite intelligent, you know, even though my behaviour doesn't bear me out—and I'd had any boy-friend I wanted. When Trent said no, and I could see that he meant it, I was utterly, totally furious.'

In spite of the younger girl's warning, Melly made a soft noise of comprehension.

'Yes,' Cathy said grimly, 'you can see what's coming, can't you? I went home and I concocted a scheme. I told you I was clever. Sir Peter and Trent were in some business deal together; I overheard my grandfather arranging to pick him up one morning. When Sir Peter arrived I was there, clad only—only in my nightdress. I threw an awful scene. I told my grandfather that he'd— that we'd—well, you know. I said that I loved Trent and I was going to marry him.'

'I see,' Melly said painfully.

'Yes. Trent denied it, of course, but I insisted. Then my grandfather made him marry me.' Here she hesitated, biting her lip. 'I don't exactly know how he managed it, but he blackmailed Trent. It was something to do with Trent's firm. A long time later my grandmother told me that Trent refused, even when Grandfather said he'd bankrupt him, but all Trent's workers would have lost their jobs, and that was what brought him around.'

Melly was sure that she had her expression well under control, but Cathy said fiercely, 'You can't despise me more than I already do, believe me. And I *didn't* know, I promise you, that he was in love with you.'

'Would it have made any difference?'

'Yes,' Cathy said simply.

Another silence while Melly tried to find a centre, some coherent chain of reasoning amidst the confused clamour of her thoughts.

'So we were married,' Cathy continued in a dead little

voice. 'I was sure that I'd be able to make him fall in love with me, but he never even touched me. Oh, I—tried. I did my best to seduce him, I tried every trick I'd read about and some I invented, but he just wasn't interested.' She laughed, a harsh sound without humour. 'He was polite—freezingly polite—he never shouted or argued, he just shut me out completely. I've never been so unhappy in my life. I realised what I'd done and that for once in my life I wasn't going to get what I wanted. When he looked at me his eyes never even saw me.'

She jumped to her feet and walked across to the window, standing for a second against the darkness outside. She looked enchanting, a fairy princess with her silky auburn hair about her shoulders and the slender, tantalising excitement of her figure. Melly swallowed hard, appreciating once more the strength of Trent's will. Whatever he thought of Cathy it must have been almost impossible at times for him to ignore her. Yet, desirable as she was, he had not touched her. Because he loved Melly Hollingworth, who was not worthy of him. Sudden stinging tears closed Melly's eyelids. She swallowed again, and when she could see once more Cathy was back in the chair.

'I know why, now,' Cathy said. 'When he looked at me he only ever saw you, of course. When my grandfather died and left Trent in control of the business I was over my infatuation, but I was still hurt and angry, so I went to live with my grandmother. I hoped he'd come after me.' She smiled wryly. 'I wanted to turn him down, you see.'

And Melly did see. Compassion overcame the bitter anger which had held her still.

'I was so young,' Cathy went on, staring at her feet. 'Not that it's any excuse, but it's the only one I can give. I told my grandmother what had happened and she was horrified. She liked Trent, she still does—did—

and he—he was so good to her after my grandfather's death, when he was working himself into the grave consolidating his position. He went on seeing her right up until . . .' Her voice trailed away for a moment, then she crossed one knee over the other, almost wriggling in the depths of the big chair, her expression softened and saddened now.

'After we'd lived apart for two years, he wanted a divorce. I told him I'd not fight him provided he didn't ever tell anyone what had happened—what I'd done.' Her lovely mouth twisted into an ugly line. 'By then I was past being angry with him. I'd grown to like him— almost like a brother. When I thought of what I'd done I was ashamed and embarrassed. But I was—I was still childish enough to want people to believe that I was the one who'd got sick of him. I didn't realise that everyone thought he'd just married me to get his hands on my grandfather's estate, how could I?'

'I should have thought,' said Melly drily, 'that it was a fairly logical assumption to make.'

'If you didn't know Trent, yes.' Cathy stared at her with something very close to hostility, and Melly bit her lip in shame.

'No one ever dared say it to me,' Cathy resumed. 'Trent isn't like that. I only lived in the same house with him for a short time, but even I know that he had the kind of integrity you bruise yourself on.'

'What made you come here tonight?'

Cathy gave a nervous little laugh. The defiance was back, sparkling angrily in the blue depths of her eyes. 'I noticed you together at that stupid party—I'd thought when I saw you in the lift together that something was going on, but I hadn't—I didn't want to think about it. Trent hasn't been himself lately. He's been—oh, bleak, distant, as if he's hurting. So I watched you at that party. Trent doesn't reveal much, he's pretty poker-faced, but once he—he looked at you as if you were his one hope of getting into heaven. And you were angry with him. I thought you must have had a quarrel, but one of my friends asked me if it made me jealous that Trent had taken up with you again.'

'She doesn't sound much like a friend.'

Cathy's shoulders moved uneasily. 'Well, I don't suppose she is, really, but she's good fun when she's not being malicious. Anyway, it doesn't matter. After she'd said that I remembered other hints and sort of snide remarks I'd heard, and I asked around a bit, and then realised that all those years ago while I'd been developing this schoolgirl crush on him he'd been in love with you. And that made me feel a lot better, because if that was so it's no wonder that he didn't want me, is it?'

She sounded so naïvely pleased with this that Melly was torn between bitter laughter and a cold anger at the results of a passionate, spoilt girl's unbridled determination to have her own way. After a short struggle the anger won.

'Three years!' she said explosively, wrenching herself to her feet to stride back and forth. 'You've wasted three years of our lives!'

Cathy shrank back. 'I know,' she said in a voice a little above a whisper. 'I'm sorry, truly I am, it's the only reason I came to see you—none of it's been much fun for me, I can assure you.'

Melly's momentary flare of anger died. 'No, I know. And I am grateful,' she said, suddenly exhausted.

'I had to come,' Cathy told her, sincerity ringing in her tones. 'I know Trent well enough to realise that he'd never tell you what had happened. He doesn't break promises. I—I want him to be happy.' Tears drowned her eyes. 'I've been so wretched,' she confided. 'But I don't think I'd have come if I hadn't realised that Trent was wretched too. And you haven't exactly been brilliant with *joie de vivre*, have you? I want you to be happy too.'

Now that it was over she got to her feet eager to be off. Slowly Melly followed her to the door, feeling as though she had been battered with rocks. She should be joyous, but as yet there was no more than a cautious lightening of the pain which had been hers for so long it was like an essential part of her personality.

'Thank you for coming,' she said a little shortly. Cathy looked down at her fingers, twisted a pretty turquoise ring, then met Melly's eyes with a slight belligerence.

'I don't suppose you mean that,' she said shrewdly. 'I must seem shallow and selfish and self-centred to you. I know I've behaved as if I am. But I am trying to improve. I'm truly sorry for what I did. I deserved to be unhappy, but you and Trent don't—didn't. My grandmother used to say that that's usually what happens when you go all out for your own ends and don't care about others. Please——' she put out a slender, pampered little hand, 'please, Melly, be happy.'

Melly took her hand and said something which must have made sense.

'I was going to tell Trent that he could tell you everything,' said Cathy as she went out of the door, 'but I could see that you needed to hear it from me. You might have thought he was making it up. You're the sort who needs to be convinced, aren't you?'

Melly nodded her head without realising what she was agreeing to, closed the door behind her surprising guest and walked slowly back into the sitting-room. Somehow Cathy's parting words hurt.

Did she need to be convinced? If Trent had told her would she have believed him? Probably not; her trust in him had been shattered so badly that only Cathy's story could have persuaded her.

She stood by the window staring unseeingly out into the light-dotted darkness, her fingers writhing together in involuntary movement while she wrestled with the question which had suddenly become critically important to her. And slowly she realised that she would have accepted anything Trent said. For one very simple reason. She had never really believed the ugly rumours which had surrounded him.

Never. Always, without consciously realising it, she had been sure that the reason for his actions was one which did him credit. That was why she still loved him; that was why she had never stopped, not even when it seemed that there was no hope.

Her teeth gnawed at her lip as she wondered now what she should do.

Her knees felt wobbly, so weak that she sat rather hurriedly in the nearest chair and began to marshal her options. Cathy had said that he still loved her, that he'd never stopped loving her. Ordinarily she would have considered Cathy too self-centred to trust her opinion, but this time Melly was inclined to believe her. Because she wanted to, quite desperately.

'What can I do?' she asked the still room despairingly. Everything had been so simple while she thought she despised him. Although she had been torn in two between her love and her principles she had at least been clear in her mind as to what she should do. But now . . .

Slowly the traffic noise faded. One of the sheep on the hill conducted a short, plaintive conversation with its lamb; long after it had ended Melly still sat motionless, her eyes fixed blankly on a particularly pleasant still-life while she tried to work out what action she should take. This time she must make the first move, for only in surrendering would she be able to satisfy Trent of her love.

And even then, she thought gravely, he would have every reason to distrust its strength. He had asked for her trust and she had mocked him; now she would have to prove it by a lifetime of loving.

Still with no plan in her head, she went to bed at last and slept heavily, waking up early to a day of brilliant sunshine. For several minutes she lay staring at a sky the colour of a Madonna's robe, deep and tender and glowing. The night had allowed her emotions to settle and she felt like the day, vivid, opening to every sensation and event with a lover's embrace.

A deep upwelling of delight suffused her whole being so that when she leaped out of the bed and caught her own eye in the mirror she was astounded at the difference. Gone was ths severity which she had assumed to be her normal aspect, the result of her too-angular features. Her eyes gleamed like black gems and her skin was flushed deeply pink over her cheekbones, all traces of sallowness fled. But the greatest difference was in her mouth. No longer firmly compressed, it tilted at the corners in a trembling, irresistible smile.

After washing her face and cleaning her teeth she drew out shorts and a T-shirt, then stood, hands stilled. A slow glimmer of humour and anticipation lit up the depths of her eyes. She replaced the clothes, taking out instead a bikini, scarlet and skimpy as the one she had worn that day at the Hornings'. In what she had later stigmatised as a moment of complete lunacy she had, the week after that day, seen this one in the window of a very exclusive and expensive little boutique, and bought it. When she had got home she had promptly stuffed it, and the cover-up which she had allowed the saleswoman to coax her into buying too, into the bottom shelf of her wardrobe. And forgotten them.

'Yes, I know it looks like a man's shirt,' the saleswoman had said. 'My dear, there's nothing more sexy than a woman in man's clothes. Roll up the sleeves—no, loosely, carelessly—yes, that's it. Now, look at yourself. Those lovely long legs, and the hint of scarlet through the fine cotton—my dear, you'll have every man in sight extremely interested!'

Now, as Melly stared at herself, she thanked that unknown woman. Through the thin white cotton the scarlet strips of the bikini gleamed with subtle attraction. Smiling, she slipped leather thongs the exact colour of the bikini on to her feet and picked up the telephone.

It took a little persuasion to coax the caretaker into using his master key on Trent's front door, and she had to lie to do it, explaining that today was Trent's birthday and she had a surprise for him.

'Well, I don't know,' he said doubtfully. 'You wouldn't get me into trouble, Miss Hollingworth, would you? Mr Addison's pretty keen on his privacy, you know.'

'I promise you, there'll be no trouble for you.'

Helped by the fact that he had seen them together—and probably by the gossip which was just as flourishing in The Towers as it was at her workplace—Melly finally managed to convince him.

'I'll meet you outside his door,' she said, trying to rein in the relief and excitement in her voice.

He grumbled a bit, and was still uneasy when she met him outside Trent's door, but after a quick survey of her laughing, glowing countenance he relaxed and opened the door for her, contenting himself with saying, 'I hope I don't lose my job over this.'

'I promise you you won't,' she returned, and he grinned and left, clearly convinced that Trent's birthday present was not in the small bag she was carrying.

Anticipation beat high in her throat, fizzed like champagne bubbles through her blood. Moving very quietly she slipped through Trent's apartment, made a quick, silent detour to the guest bathroom, then walked purposefully through the sitting room out on to the terrace.

The shrubs and trees were still heavy with dew, the huge scarlet amaryllis like blazing torches in the sun.

For long moments Melly stood, eyes caught by the view, the long arms of the harbour glittering silver, the fresh joyous youth of the day, the laughter of the sun over the city and the parks and the sea. Even the satyr with his cynical, worldly gaze seemed young again.

Then she pulled the shirt over her head, slid her feet free of the thongs and dived into the pool.

The water was a shock to her system, but after several lengths she had warmed up and was striking out fiercely, using her best crawl stroke, swimming away the cold voice in her brain that kept trying to tell her that she was a fool.

So determined was she to pay no attention to it that the hand around her ankle came as an unpleasant and startling surprise. She gulped a mouthful of water and sank, choking and coughing as she was hauled upright against Trent's lean chest, her eyes streaming.

'Oh, you beast!' she gasped, pushing ineffectually against him.

His chuckle reverberated against the palms of her hands. Shyly she pushed her hair out of her eyes and looked up into his face. He was laughing, but the grey eyes were very warm and tender.

Water cascaded from the dark, muscular breadth of his shoulders, glittered, then dried on his distinctive features. He looked so magnificent that Melly's mouth dried and she had to stand there looking up at him in silent supplication.

'Is that a nice way to greet your lover?' he asked lightly as his hands slid across her back.

'You're not——'

'You've come to me. That makes you mine. My lover, my wife, my darling, my own . . .' His proud head blocked the sun as his mouth covered hers. Without thought, wanting only to make up for the past years, she opened her lips beneath his in mute invitation.

An invitation Trent was not slow in accepting. She

had expected a hard and hungry passion, prepared for it and would have welcomed it, for he was hers and she loved him, and she knew that his love for her had become tinted by anger and frustration. But as his mouth touched hers she realised that he was being gentle with her, revealing more than any words how tenderly he loved her.

The only indication of the strength of his emotions was the arms which bound her so tightly that it took her a minute or so to appreciate that he had not bothered to put a swimsuit on. A sensuous little thrill activated her nerve-ends. She pressed herself eagerly against him, her mouth curving into a smile beneath his.

'You're shivering,' he said vaguely.

'Mmm.' But when he went to put her away from him she wound her arms tightly around his waist and refused to let go.

A long time later he said on a note of laughter and passion, 'Making love al fresco has its moments, but you're starting to feel like a frog, all cold and clammy. Come in and I'll make you some breakfast.'

Breakfast was not exactly what Melly had in mind, but she let him go and allowed herself to be hauled out of the pool. But instead of releasing her Trent began to kiss her again. The bronze nymph smiled benignly on them; even the satyr seemed to have lost a little of his habitual cynicism as he watched the long fierce kisses, desperate with a hunger too long denied.

'Oh God,' Trent muttered against her mouth, the deep voice rough with emotion, 'Melly, my darling girl, I love you so much that I'm unhinged with wanting. Can we get married as soon as possible? It only takes three days to get a licence ... Do you want to be married at Te Puriri? Jennet has everything organised. All she needs is a definite date.'

'You have been busy!' But she wasn't annoyed; she rather thought she would never be annoyed again.

Glints of mockery and desire heated the ice-grey eyes. 'Yes. I've done everything properly. I asked your brother for your hand when he was down.'

'Rafe?' Melly was awed. 'The rotten beast! He never said a word!'

Trent grinned, enormously pleased with himself. 'I asked him not to. He was a bit stiff at first, but he unbent. I rather got the idea that he'd been the recipient of occasional confidences from you.'

'He had,' she said in a voice whose grimness was totally belied by the sensuous tracking of her fingers through the wet hair at the nape of his neck. 'It's beginning to sound rather like a conspiracy!'

'Only a little one.'

She laughed and lifted her face to bite the lobe of his ear, very gently, very swiftly. 'You don't have to wait for a wedding,' she whispered into it. 'When I came in I put my toothbrush and a few essentials into your second bathroom. It's a wonder you didn't hear me.'

He said absently, 'That's probably what woke me up.' Then, as she traced the line of his ear with the tip of her tongue, he put a stern hand beneath her chin and said, 'No!'

But he met the bemused passion in her expression with a groan. As if she made it impossible for him to keep any sort of control his mouth crushed hers beneath it and he undid the ties of her bikini and pulled her free of the scarlet scraps of material and picked her up.

Not to the bedroom—he stopped just inside the huge glass doors and laid her on the carpet and gently, tenderly, possessed himself again of all that he desired, his broken love words heating her blood, his hands worshipping the lines and planes and curves of her body until her passion matched his. Then, aflame with a kind of sensual magic, she pulled him into her and a white heat of erotic sensation joined them.

Afterwards, a lifetime afterwards, she told him ruefully, 'I feel as though I've run a marathon. You don't know your own strength.'

Trent smiled, that slashing feral smile that sparked a wild repsonse deep within her. 'Oh, I know it,' he said. 'It's your own fault you get bruised. You shouldn't be so desirable that I lose all control.'

'I don't mind,' Melly said lightly, pouring coffee into two large china mugs. She was so attuned, so responsive that every tiny sensation seemed magnified. The sun flooded the kitchen in a warm golden glow, the coffee smelled and tasted like nectar, the strawberries Trent had hulled for her breakfast were tangy and sharp and sweet. He even had yoghurt in the fridge. He raised an eyebrow at her sudden smile, so she kissed him and was pulled down into his lap.

'You taste of grapefruit,' she teased.

'You taste of heaven.'

She blushed. 'You say such charming things!'

'I mean them.' His strong, lean hand closed over hers. 'What made you decide to surrender, my love!'

'Cathy came to see me last night.'

This surprised him. For a moment the bleak hardness returned to his face. His hand tightened over hers as he said without expression, 'I see. Given time, I think she'll overcome that unfortunate upbringing of hers.'

'I'm sure she will. It took all her courage to see me, but she said she thought she had to. She said that she'd have released you from your promise not to tell, only she knew I wouldn't believe you.' Melly lifted troubled eyes. 'Trent, I would have.'

'I know.'

She gave a small, ironic smile. 'I felt very small. I sat for ages in the dark and went over the whole situation until I realised that I'd never really given up on you. I just thought I had.'

'I know that,' he said comfortingly. 'When we met in

the lift that day it was like being kicked in the stomach, but I knew immediately that you still loved me.'

'How?' she asked. 'You were—rather horrible, and I wasn't in the least nice to you.'

'Because you are my other half,' he said calmly. 'I felt your response as if it was mine. Pain, anger, contempt—and beneath it a great surge of joy and relief. Just as I felt.'

'I see.' The words came slowly, underlined with wonder. 'So you——'

'I knew I was going to pursue you until I had you where you belong.'

'In your bed?'

The grey eyes glinted with laughter and desire, but he shook his head. 'In my heart, the centre point of my life.'

'I didn't really believe the rumours, but I told myself I did.'

'I know. You used them as a shield, hiding yourself behind it in case you got hurt again.'

He removed the hand which had been so warm around hers and drank some of his coffee, setting the cup down to continue, 'When Cathy pulled her trick I could have killed her. She was a spoilt, totally self-centred brat, and I refused to give in to that very unsubtle blackmail. Sir Peter, the old devil, was besotted by her, he thought she could do no wrong. He saw me as a brutal betrayer.'

'You don't have to tell me,' Melly said quietly.

'Just this once, then we'll not think of it again.'

The black brows drew together and he frowned, then stared into his coffee mug. 'Unfortunately, he had the power to make me do what he wanted to.' Almost imploringly he looked up at her. 'Melissa, at that time I'd put my future and almost every cent I'd had into the business. Sir Peter controlled the only supplier of the disc storage unit we used. He had the power to withhold supplies. If it had been just me he threatened I'd have told him to go to hell; I'm not good blackmail material. But if I'd done that, I'd have had to spend an immense amount of money I didn't have just to buy alternative supplies and at least half of the work force would have had to be laid off. I couldn't do it. Those people needed their jobs. So I—gave in.'

'You were right,' she said softly. 'Of course you were right. Knowing you, there was nothing else you could do.'

'Power has obligations,' Trent said drily, 'and responsibilities. I had to surrender, although it nearly killed me to see Cathy's smug little face and Sir Peter's satisfaction. But the worst thing was that letter I wrote to you. I wanted to make you hate me so that you'd get over me more quickly.'

'Fat hope,' she said under her breath.

'Did it hurt?'

She gave him a wry smile. 'Yes, it hurt.'

The harsh lines of his face tightened. 'Yes, well, I didn't get married in a very good mood and I wasn't inclined to be easy on Cathy. It probably would have been less stressful for both of us if I'd treated her as a conniving, deceitful little cheat—but hell, she was only a spoilt schoolgirl. She had no idea of what she'd done. She was still living in a romantic dream.' He paused. 'Not for long, though. With the best will in the world I couldn't do more than to be polite to her. I told you the truth when I said I'd never touched her.'

'And I believed you,' said Melly, adding guiltily, 'I tried to convince myself that you'd left her alone because the rumours were true, you'd only married her to get your hands on Durrants'. For a while I thought I believed it.'

Trent nodded and drained his coffee, setting the cup back on the table and turning it with his long fingers. 'You made that quite obvious! Believe me, I cursed myself for letting you get to me so hard that I had to try to justify myself, even if it was in that small way.'

His fingers stilled, moved to clasp her hand. He leant his cheek into her breast in the age-old gesture of one who seeks comfort. Both were silent, recalling that incident and its aftermath.

'I wish I could say that I was sorry for taking you,' he said at last, his arm tightening about her, 'but I must admit that I enjoyed every minute of it. I've loved you for so long, been incomplete without you; I behaved without any restraint at all, but oh God, I needed that surrender so much! I'm sorry I was so rough—I honestly thought you'd experimented with sex before you came back.'

'Are you sorry I hadn't?' she asked slyly, lowering her cheek on to his hair so that he wouldn't see the sweep of colour rise from her throat.

She felt his cheek move against her breast as he smiled. 'If I tell you that the knowledge that I'm your first lover, your only lover, makes me feel like Alexander the Great, will you lecture me about the double standard?'

'I think you know about it already.'

'I do, I do, and my brain agrees that what's sauce for the gander is definitely sauce for the goose. I've never been hung up on virginity before, never cared how many lovers any woman I'd wanted had had. But you— you're special. When I think of you I revert right back to primitive. Mine, I think, and God help anyone who tries to take her away from me!' Trent laughed softly, scoffing at his own surprised atavism and ran a leisurely possessive hand from her knee to the soft warm skin on the inside of her thigh.

'Don't!' she gasped, trying to escape from those probing, too-knowing fingers. She wore nothing beneath her shirt; if she turned her head she could see through the window the tiny scarlet heaps which were the pieces of her bikini.

'Do you want to fly up to Te Puriri?' Trent asked, setting her on the floor with a slap across her backside. 'If I ring Mangere now we could be up there in an hour and half. Would you like to drop in on Rafe and Jennet and tell them to start preparing for a wedding in, say, a fornight?'

'I'd love to!' she laughed. 'Mind you, Jen will kill us! So little time . . .'

'Am I rushing you?' he asked anxiously as he got to his feet. 'Would you rather wait and have a proper wedding wth eight bridesmaids and all the trimmings?'

'Don't be an idiot,' she said with immense tenderness, sliding her arms around his waist. Her mouth turned into his throat. Against her lips she felt the strong beat of his pulse. 'I've waited long enough. Years and years and years and years. I'm afraid that if I don't marry you as quickly as possible someone else will decide to blackmail you, or kidnap you, or——'

'Or nothing,' he interrupted. 'Nothing is ever going to take you away from me, nothing and nobody. I wouldn't have been able to do it last time if you hadn't been half a world away.'

'And if you hadn't been so concerned about the welfare of your employees,' said Melly softly.

He shrugged as if disclaiming the praise, but she knew that it was that strong protective streak in him that had led him into marriage. It was that same instinct to protect which kept him looking after Cathy now, giving her the support she needed while she tried to find some direction for her life. There would be occasions when Melly would wonder just why she had to put up with Cathy's presence, but all jealousy was gone. She could even admire the girl. It had taken courage of a particularly gritty sort to admit what she had done, but she had done it, and done it, moreover, with a certain dignity.

'As for blackmail,' Trent interrupted her thoughts by

saying, 'you can forget about it. I know you've always considered me to be a pirate, but with that power you despise so much there comes a certain immunity to the sort of shoddy tactics Cathy used. This time nothing is going to prevent me from claiming you. I like this shirt, incidentally, especially the way you're wearing it now.'

The sudden change of direction in the conversation made Melly gasp and then laugh. When she told him what the saleswoman in the boutique had said he grinned, obviously agreeing. His hands took the weight of her breasts, tormenting her with a thousand stimulating pleasure pangs.

'If that volcano,' he said, apparently not realising that he was undoing the buttons of the shirt, 'decided to burst into flames right now, we'd die together, because I'm not letting you out of my sight until I have you signed, sealed and delivered.'

By now she was naked again and he was looking down at what his hands had revealed. Melly stood, acquiescent, almost submissive, until she lifted her eyes and met the glittering possession of his.

'Are you insatiable?' she asked huskily.

'Seem to be. Let's find out, shall we?'

'Te Puriri?'

He chuckled deep in his throat. 'Oh, to hell with it! We'll ring them up later. How would you like to live in sin for a few days until we come up for air?'

'I thought I was,' she said reproachfully. 'Living in sin, I mean, not coming up for air. I told you I brought my toothbrush. That was as good as a declaration.'

'I do love you.' He kissed her, then lifted his head to stare down into the rapt, bemused face framed by his hands. Slowly the flame in his eyes died. He gave a sudden impeded groan and hauled her fiercely against him, burying his face in her curls, holding her in a grip so hard that it hurt.

'Darling,' he muttered, 'oh, darling, it's been hell!

Wanting you, *needing* you so badly, and all the time
knowing I'd made you hate me. I felt sorry for Cathy,
she was bitterly unhappy, but I couldn't bear the sight
of her. Every time I looked at her I thought, because of
you, Melissa hates me, and it took all of my self-
control not to hit her across her pretty, pampered little
face. I hated her. I didn't dare lose control in case I
killed her.'

'Oh, Trent! You had the worst of it, my darling.'

He shrugged and the bitter savagery in his expression
faded. 'She didn't enjoy life much either. When she
came to her senses she did what she could to mend
things. She told Sir Peter what she'd done.'

'Good.' Melly was rarely vindictive, but her voice
was fierce as she continued, 'I hope it made him feel like
a swine! Playing God . . .'

'She was the light of his old age, but the old devil
didn't really think much of women. He treated them
like toys, even Cathy. He was sorry he'd listened to her,
but he thought I should just make the best of it. He told
me she'd make a good wife. All she needed, he said, was
a touch of the stick now and then to bring her to heel.'

Melly stiffened, horrified. That cynical note she hated
had made its appearance in his voice and she was
repelled by it, and by Sir Peter's outlook on marriage.

'I'm glad you didn't agree,' she said in muted tones.

Trent laughed and the lonely cynicism died as he
looked down into her face, his gaze fixing on the soft,
ardent curve of her mouth. 'He was quite without
scruples, the old tyrant. He thought mine were a
weakness. Not that he was averse to making use of them.'

'What do you mean?' queried Melly.

A million nerves in her body shivered into delight as
his hands began to stroke a sensuous path down her
spine.

'He asked me to look after her. That's why I see her
so often.'

'It must have been difficult for you, after the separation.' She was rather pleased at how objective her voice sounded.

'Oh, it was.' His hands measured her waist, lingered over the satin skin above with loving persistence. 'But I welcomed it. I knew I had to wait two years before I could divorce her. Coping with Sir Peter's empire gave me something to fill the time with.'

'You—didn't know I'd come back,' she said, shaken. 'No?'

'*No.*' The black curls trembled as she lifted her face to scan his. 'What if I'd married over there?'

Trent grinned, that fierce, predatory pirate's grin. 'Then I'd have seduced you away from your husband.'

'And you've just told me you have scruples!' She hid her shock with the rallying statement, but she was oddly unsurprised.

'Not where you're concerned.' He made it sound like a vow. 'You still don't understand, do you? You and I—we belong. I'd have broken up your marriage, even if you'd been happy, I'm ruthless enough to do anything to make you mine. If it had been twenty years before I was free I'd have come after you. Why do you think I bought this place? I knew Rafe owned an apartment in it; I was making sure I had every advantage I might possibly need. You've called me a pirate more than once, Melissa. What you don't seem to understand is that I am, and you are my treasure.'

He laughed, a sound without humour, and his hands moved swiftly, fiercely, to her hips.

'*Mine,*' he emphasied, his eyes clear and blazing into her face. 'Always mine, from the moment I realised that I loved you.'

Melly slid her arms around his neck, offering herself to him, her mind suddenly clear. 'And you,' she said quietly, 'are mine.'

He laughed, swinging her around in the warm

sunshine, love and something that surely was not relief relaxing the contours of his face.

'Good,' he said with immense satisfaction. 'Now, let's get ready and go. I've decided that I'll feel a lot more confident that I've really got you at last when we've told your family and made it official.'

'No living in sin?'

He laughed at the mock-disappointment of her expression. 'No. We pirates suffer from a deep-rooted insecurity that makes us very keen on outward and visible chains—gold ones, like wedding rings and marriage lines. They reassure us.'

She gave a choked little laugh. 'Pirates always went for tangible treasure, didn't they? I don't believe you, Trent. If you were like that you'd have made the best of Cathy and forgotten all about me.'

'I suppose so.' He let her go and watched as she pulled the shirt on and began to button it up. 'Well, I couldn't. Perhaps I'm not your average buccaneer after all. All I know is that I've never been so happy in my life since I saw you walking across the lobby towards the lift. I knew then that without you my life just wasn't worth the effort.'

Her fingers faltered, then stopped. 'It's—frightening, isn't it?' she said soberly, watching him with something like trepidation.

The predatory buccaneer's face lit up with anticipation. 'Frightening?' he scorned. 'No, my darling, it's the most exciting thing in the whole world! You and me, girl, that's it. That's the greatest gamble we'll ever face, and we face it knowing we're going to win! What could be more exciting than that?'

And she believed him, walking by his side into their future with all of his fierce confidence to guide them.

Coming Next Month

943 ISHBEL'S PARTY Stacy Absalom
A peaceful Suffolk village seems the perfect place for a nurse to recover from injuries, but for the presence of the man she lost that awful night of Ishbel's party—the man she still loves.

944 THE PUPPET MASTER Pippa Clarke
The man who's trying to close down her sister's Mediterranean restaurant might be the puppet master, but Anna is no willing marionette. Still, seeing him with his ex-lover does tug at her heartstrings.

945 ADAM'S LAW Claudia Jameson
A domineering sculptor tries to bully an injured model back to life, back to her glamorous career in the city. But she'd miss life in Guernsey and the love she's found there.

946 DESIRE NEVER CHANGES Penny Jordan
The daughter of a British ambassador is shocked when a world-renowned photographer threatens to expose compromising photos he took of her five years ago—unless she agrees to marry him!

947 IMPACT Madeleine Ker
A young woman meeting her fiancé's best friend for the first time is confused when he tries to turn her against the man she's promised to marry—especially since she knows he's right.

948 BODYCHECK Elizabeth Oldfield
Attraction flares between a model and her bodyguard in Paris. Yet she's afraid to break things off with her boyfriend, even though she appears to be a "good-time girl" dangling two men on the line.

949 ELUSIVE PARADISE Lilian Peake
"Who'll be prince to my Cinderella?" a researcher asks at her friend's wedding reception, never expecting her new boss to answer in earnest. Why, his reputation for dealing ruthlessly with staff is legend.

950 TIME FOR ANOTHER DREAM Karen van der Zee
Indecision plagues a young widow after she convinces the head of a sheltered workshop in Virginia that she isn't a flighty socialite. Her thoughts about her new boss have definitely turned to fancy.

Available in January wherever paperback books are sold, or through Harlequin Reader Service:

In the U.S.
P.O. Box 1397
Buffalo, N.Y.
14240-1397

In Canada
P.O. Box 603
Fort Erie, Ontario
L2A 9Z9

ATTRACTIVE, SPACE SAVING BOOK RACK

Display your most prized novels on this handsome and sturdy book rack. The hand-rubbed walnut finish will blend into your library decor with quiet elegance, providing a practical organizer for your favorite hard-or soft-covered books.

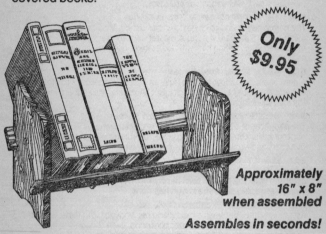

Only $9.95

Approximately 16" x 8" when assembled

Assembles in seconds!

To order, rush your name, address and zip code, along with a check or money order for $10.70* ($9.95 plus 75¢ postage and handling) payable to *Harlequin Reader Service*:

Harlequin Reader Service
Book Rack Offer
901 Fuhrmann Blvd.
P.O. Box 1325
Buffalo, NY 14269-1325

Offer not available in Canada.

*New York residents add appropriate sales tax.

BKR-1R

Can you keep a secret?

You can keep this one plus 4 free novels

Here's how to get this special offer from Harlequin!
As simple as 1...2...3!

1. Each month, save one Treasury Edition coupon from your favorite Romance or Presents novel.
2. In four months you'll have saved four Treasury Edition coupons (only one coupon per month allowed).
3. Then all you have to do is fill out and return the order form provided, along with the four Treasury Edition coupons required and $2.95 for postage and handling.

Mail to: Harlequin Reader Service

In the U.S.A.
901 Fuhrmann Blvd.
P.O. Box 1397
Buffalo, NY 14240

In Canada
P.O. Box 609
Fort Erie, Ontario
L2A 9Z9

BN-Dec-2

Please send me my Special copy of the Betty Neels Treasury Edition. I have enclosed the four Treasury Edition coupons required and $2.95 for postage and handling along with this order form. (Please Print)

NAME_____

ADDRESS_____

CITY_____

STATE/PROV._____ ZIP/POSTAL CODE_____

SIGNATURE_____

This offer is limited to one order per household.

This special Betty Neels offer expires
February 28, 1987.

SUPPLIES LIMITED

...great collection. The first eight titles
...mplete and mail this coupon today to
order books you may have missed.

Harlequin Reader Service

In U.S.A.
901 Fuhrmann Blvd.
P.O. Box 1397
Buffalo, N.Y. 14140

In Canada
P.O. Box 2800
Postal Station A
5170 Yonge Street
Willowdale, Ont. M2N 6J3

Please send me the following titles from the Janet Dailey Americana
Collection. I am enclosing a check or money order for $2.75 for each
book ordered, plus 75¢ for postage and handling.

_____	ALABAMA	Dangerous Masquerade
_____	ALASKA	Northern Magic
_____	ARIZONA	Sonora Sundown
_____	ARKANSAS	Valley of the Vapours
_____	CALIFORNIA	Fire and Ice
_____	COLORADO	After the Storm
_____	CONNECTICUT	Difficult Decision
_____	DELAWARE	The Matchmakers

Number of titles checked @ $2.75 each = $_____

N.Y. RESIDENTS ADD
   APPROPRIATE SALES TAX $_____

Postage and Handling $ .75

                              TOTAL $_____

I enclose _____

(Please send check or money order. We cannot be responsible for cash
sent through the mail.)

PLEASE PRINT

NAME _____

ADDRESS _____

CITY _____

STATE/PROV. _____